About the Author

Andrew Bullas was born in Worcestershire. After a BA in Fine Art from Portsmouth Polytechnic he attended The London Film School. Subsequently he has divided his time between independent film-making, teaching and a stint working for the film archive of The Imperial War Museum. He is the founder of Pepwell Productions, and his first novel, *Charlie Echo*, is also published by Matador.

THE GLEAM OF CLEAR WATER

ANDREW BULLAS

Matador
Unit E2 Airfield Business Park
Harrison Road, Market Harborough
Leicestershire LE16 7UL
Tel: 0116 279 2299
Email: books@troubador.co.uk
Web: www.troubador.co.uk/matador
Twitter: @matadorbooks

ISBN 9781805140306

'Messing About on The River'
Tony Hatch © Dejamus Ltd 1961
Lyrics reproduced courtesy of Dejamus Ltd.

British Library Cataloguing in Publication Data.
A catalogue record for this book is available from the British Library.

Printed by TJ Books Ltd, Padstow, UK
Typeset in 11pt Minion Pro by Troubador Publishing Ltd, Leicester, UK

Matador is an imprint of Troubador Publishing Ltd

When Sir Percival came nigh to the brim,
and saw the water so boisterous,
He doubted to overpass it.

Sir Thomas Mallory

Preface

I ONCE FOUND MYSELF LIVING IN ARNOLD BENNETT'S old house. More than that, living in the room he used to write in. Not that I knew it at the time of taking the tenancy. I was simply looking for somewhere cheap and a sign in the newsagent's window had led to 9, Fulham Park Gardens.

It was only later that the landlady explained the literary association. Apparently, AB had described the view from the window where he put pen to paper, remarking on the Poplar trees in the garden and the tube line running along the embankment at the end of it, all of which were still present in the mid 1990s.

Although I'd never read a word of the man's prodigious output, general knowledge had acquainted me with two facts: one, that he was a fellow Midlander, and two, that the British 1950s comedy film *The Card* had been based on one of his novels. Sparse though it was, this information was enough to add a modest aura to digs which were, in fact, pretty cramped.

The two sash windows helped though, the one that

faced the railway line and the other which afforded a view of the Pickfords' furniture removal depot next door, and on warm summer nights, when both were open to their fullest extent, it was possible to lie in bed and listen to messages coming into the drivers' cabs whilst they were halted at the railway signal just a few yards away. Were there any other messages during my tenure there I wonder? Profound insights about writing or choice words of encouragement from the previous resident? Nope! Don't think so. Sure, there were vibrations, but only the ones coming from District Line trains rumbling back and forth. Nevertheless, this book was begun in that room and latter-day research did reveal a couple of further parallels between AB #1 and AB #2. It seems that it was mainly journalism that occupied Bennett during his time in London SW6. Bread and butter work if you like, but no doubt providing a valuable groundwork for the popular novels that were to be written after he'd moved on to grander addresses elsewhere. And, whilst I make no claims for being either journalist or novelist, I do recognise the importance of doing the groundwork and the objective, as personified by the hero of *The Card*, namely, "*the great cause of cheering us all up.*"

January 2023

Chapter One

H E SAW THE TRUCK BEFORE HE HEARD IT – A cloud of dust spreading like rust along a cheap pen knife.

No stainless steel in this town, he thought, as he glanced down at the corrugated iron roofs below, *just dust and decay.* The only thing that shone brightly was the idea that had taken root in his mind, an idea that he was now, despite the risks, determined to follow.

Slowly he lowered himself down the ladder of the wind pump. It was the only speed he could move at anyway, his two broken ribs and torn muscles made sure of that. Besides, any rapid movement might catch the attention of the passengers in the truck. As he descended further, the skeletal structure of the girders blended with the branches of the dead trees eliminating any further risk of detection.

Despite his measured pace, sweat was pouring off him by the time he reached the house. So, grabbing a shirt from the back of a chair, he towelled himself dry before putting it on and doing up a couple of buttons. That done, he pulled a baseball cap down low over his eyes and walked out onto the porch. Whatever else, no one could say he hadn't made an effort to look smart!

The truck pulled up, its black paintwork caked with the orange dust characteristic of that part of Western Australia, and a wiry kid hopped down from the driver's side.

"Hi, Laurie," the man in the sweaty shirt called as he watched the kid make his way to the rear of the vehicle and lower the tail gate.

"The name's Lawrence," the kid shot back moodily.

"Ah, so it's *Lawrence* now, is it?"

The kid hoisted two boxes of groceries into his arms and ferried them past the man in the sweaty shirt and into the house.

"What's up with him?" asked the man, turning to the second visitor to emerge from the cab.

"Tony's officially promoted him to driver, only he doesn't like having to wash the truck after every trip we make out here."

"Those shiny baubles sure show up the dust, don't they?"

"Seemed like they might've turned your head too, once upon a time."

"Once upon a time was a *long, long* time ago," the man in the sweaty shirt replied, teeth showing white through his dark beard. "No point getting all beat up over a few coats of new paint."

The visitor grunted in agreement and looked deeper into the smiling face searching for clues as to its owner's mental state. It wasn't easy because so much of it was obscured by the cap and extensive facial hair.

"You sound like an old man."

"I feel like one."

The bantering tone was the default setting between them, so no tell-tale signs there.

"Alright; Grandpa, on that rocker while I look at your stitches."

The man in the sweaty shirt retreated to the porch, sat on a rickety old chair and allowed the older man to raise the baseball cap and examine his left eyebrow. Experienced fingers moved around the puffy skin as he did so.

"Seems to be healing pretty well. Might leave a scar or two, but don't worry, they'll be lost amongst the wrinkles."

The man in the sweaty shirt smiled again, making him appear much closer to his real age which was all of twenty-four.

"Got any mail for me, Spence?" he asked, replacing his baseball cap.

"Bits and pieces."

The older man was just handing over a bunch of envelopes when they heard footsteps approaching.

"Best open them after we've gone though, eh?" he added conspiratorially and the man in the sweaty shirt nodded.

"There's soap and deodorant on the kitchen table, why don't you try using them sometime, *Percival?*" the kid sneered as he strolled past.

"Because the water smells worse than I do," the man in the sweaty shirt shot back.

"That's hard to believe."

"Less of your lip, Lol," growled the man in the sweaty shirt who, for obvious reasons, much preferred being called Perc to Percival.

"It's probably mineral deposits," interjected Spencer, playing referee. "After all, the place was a mining town years ago. Pipes probably got cracked between times and some bad stuff started seeping in."

"Well, he'd better do something about the old personal hygiene soon, cos he's not getting in my truck reeking like that. He'll be walking back to Perth, instead."

"Getting a bit precious, aren't we, Lawrence?"

"I've got standards that's all."

"You've got attitude, is all, but I'll soon knock that out of you."

Perc was halfway up from his chair before Spencer landed a restraining hand on his shoulder.

"Easy, Perc. Easy!"

It was a simple gesture and a simple phrase, but it brought back powerful memories for both of them. Right from the start of their association, Spencer had always insisted Perc sit out the entire ring break between rounds, never allowing him to jump off his stool early and use up precious energy on showy theatrics. "Save your energy for what matters," had been his mantra, a tough one for a naturally hot-headed young fighter like Perc Morgan to follow, but it had served him well when he had, both inside the ring and out of it, and the trainer didn't see any reason to change his methods now.

Sensing Perc relax again, Spencer returned his attention to the kid. "Off-load the diesel for the generator and I'll meet you out front in five minutes, okay?"

The kid hesitated.

"Okay?" Spencer asked again more forcefully.

"Okay," the kid mumbled before sloping outside.

"Well, the reactions are still pretty good, for an old timer that is. Now show me the ribs."

Perc pulled the shirt up from his hip.

"Such formality all of a sudden? First the cap and now a shirt too. I'm amazed you didn't put on a tie, just to round it all off."

Perc inclined his head in the direction the kid had just taken. "Prying eyes."

The trainer grunted in acknowledgment, which encouraged Perc to elaborate further.

"I figure I got busted up by following someone else's schedule, so now I'm going to heal by following my own. No more rushing things. And just because the bruises have almost gone… "

"Yeah, the kid would be sure to mention that much," the older man agreed, letting the shirt fall again.

"But either way, I wouldn't count on postponing the royal summons much longer."

"How long?"

"Three days. A week maybe, then the spa break's over.

Perc frowned.

"So, the way I see it, you and the kid might just as well start trying to get along," continued the older man as he moved out from under the shade of the porch. "All this constant bitchin' is driving me nuts."

Perc made a deliberate show of tucking his shirt into the waist band of his trousers before responding. "Alright, Spence."

"What, no arguments?" said the older man doing a double take.

"Maybe you are still suffering from concussion after all!"

"He didn't knock me out, Spence. He just shook me up a little."

"Right," said Spencer, brushing away a fly.

"Thing is," Perc continued a tad awkwardly, "the kid's right!"

Spencer's penetrating gaze was back on him in a flash.

"Well, about one thing, anyway."

"Go on."

"I *do* need to get clean, but I want clean water to do it with. I've been using all the bottles you guys bring for drinking, but I tell you, Spence, and it's the weirdest thing, but almost as soon as I got here, I started dreaming about the stuff. Can you believe that? I dream about water! Every night and often during the daytime as well, vast expanses of the stuff stretching away into the distance. Pure, clear water all there just for the taking. It's like a mirage, only you can't *dream* a mirage can you? It's a contradiction in terms, right?"

Trainer stared at fighter for a long time before stepping off what remained of the wooden steps onto the dusty track. He'd always had misgivings about sending Perc so far out from the city.

Sure, it made sense to keep him away from press and TV cameras hungry for a shot of boxing's latest golden boy suddenly not looking so golden anymore. But sequestering him in a disused mining town smacked of lazy thinking on management's part; the clearest signal yet that Perc was just another asset to be bundled together with the rest of the property portfolio. Put out to pasture like an injured racehorse. Excepting that, even a broken down moke[1] would've been hard pressed to find a blade of

---

1   Australian slang for an inferior horse.

grass out here. Yet, all things considered, Perc didn't seem to be brooding too much and, crucially, his subconscious appeared to be playing a useful part in the recovery process as well. Something Spencer felt it might be beneficial to encourage.

"Maybe it was the water that was dreaming you," he said at last.

"How's that, Spence?"

Spencer paused again. His First Nation people's heritage was something he seldom discussed with foreigners, yet something about the present situation persuaded him to persist and, bending down, he began drawing a series of concentric circles in the dirt with his finger.

"The emblem for water or water hole," he said once he'd finished.

"The dreamings emerge from it and enter into it as well, understand?"

Perc leant in closer. "Which lines are meant to be the dreams and which ones the water?"

Spencer shook his head and wondered if he hadn't made a mistake in sharing the symbol after all.

"If it's too literal it loses its power, right?"

"Right," the younger man agreed, but he didn't sound too sure.

"So, they all become the same element."

"Lines, dreams, water, everything?"

"Lines, dreams, water, *everything*," said Spencer, rising to his feet once more.

"Deep," mused the young man as the emblem embedded itself in his mind's eye.

"And far too, maybe," added Spencer tellingly.

"Like a quest, maybe?"

"Maybe."

They were both still staring at the marks in the dust when the truck drove up, obliterating Spencer's handiwork in an instant. A cocky young voice shouted above the radio and, scant seconds later, Perc was left alone to ponder what it all meant.

Chapter Two

THE MURKY WATERS OF THE RIVER THAMES LAPPED rhythmically over the gravel, whilst somewhere nearby a church clock struck eight. Further up the embankment, the shapes of assorted clubhouses were slowly emerging through the morning mist. A solitary road sweeper pushed his truck along the roadway, the fluorescent green of his jacket glowing strangely in the diffused light. Then, as if on cue, the doors to one of the clubhouses opened and several crew members began taking their rowing blades down to the water, shivering as they went. Two others then followed, dragging a launch down the slope, while a third, Perc, now clean shaven and properly kitted out, lugged down the outboard motor without too much visible effort. The average age of the group appeared to be mid to late twenties with one man, Dave, the coach, carrying several more years and pounds than the rest. "Is she reliable, this friend of yours?" he asked one of the group, with a soft Scottish burr.

"She's a colleague, not a friend," replied a slightly anxious figure, flapping his arms in a vain attempt to keep warm.

"She must be a *very* good colleague to agree to try her hand at coxing," a beefy guy muttered with a wink and Geordie accent.

"Just up for a challenge, I guess," replied the first man cagily and whose name happened to be Neil.

"Or maybe she was just pissed when you asked her?"

"She doesn't drink, well, not that I know of, anyway," said Neil, feeling increasingly uncomfortable.

"They usually do," reflected Dave with a smile containing the wisdom of the ages.

Not so far away, a car pulled up at a set of traffic lights and the driver, who was Chinese and pretty, tried to examine the map on the passenger seat beside her. However, an angry toot from an impatient driver behind soon prompted her blindly onwards again.

Meanwhile, outside the boathouse, a veteran club member was examining a beautiful old wooden sculling boat that was resting on a pair of trestles. He looked up disapprovingly as Dave approached and made to make friendly. "You got your boat back then, Leonard?"

"What?" asked the veteran whose generally grumpy manner wasn't helped by serious hearing loss.

"Your boat, you got it fixed," continued Dave more loudly.

"What?"

Dave sighed and lifted the loud hailer he was carrying to his mouth. "Mended!"

"Yes, cost me four hundred bloody pounds too!"

Dave lifted the megaphone once more and tried to look

encouraging. "Well, you should be alright this morning, the river's nice and quiet."

Leonard did not reply but looked past the coach to where a shiny, new BMW was parking.

"We'll find out, wont we?" he replied, unconvinced.

Hannah, the driver of the vehicle, was just about to get out when Neil hurried over to her.

"You made it!"

"Afraid I wouldn't show up?"

"No."

"Liar."

"Only I wouldn't park just there, if I were you."

"Why? I am not blocking anyone, am I?"

"It's the river," interjected Dave, ambling over. "When the tide rises it'll wash your car away."

The woman glanced down to the water's edge, but even though it was a considerable distance away, there was an unmistakable note of anxiety in her voice when she spoke again.

"Surely it won't come in as high as this?"

"Oh, you'd be surprised what it can do," smiled the coach.

Taking their collective warnings seriously, she manoeuvred into a safer spot before getting out. It was only then that she became aware of all the appraising stares directed at her. The stares were not intended to be intimidating, although no doubt they felt that way to her. The men were just not prepared to see someone so petite. Someone, in other words, so physically perfect for the role they each hoped she was going to play in their collective sporting destiny.

In fact, she cut a smart figure all round. The track suit, the way the dark hair was neatly tied back and the pearl earrings, ill-suited to the bite of an English winter morning though they might be, did nothing to diminish their collective approval. In other words, she hadn't merely arrived, she had made an entrance.

"Dave, this is Hannah," Neil announced, placing a hand on her shoulder. "Dave'll tell you what to do."

Something about the gesture jarred with Perc, who happened to be walking back to the boathouse at that moment. It was something his manager, Anthony, used to do to him whenever the pair of them appeared at press conferences or weigh-ins before a fight. At the start of his pro career, it had felt like an act of solidarity, a reminder that Anthony literally had his back and was looking out for him. However, standing there on the tideway that cold January day, it struck him that the old hand on the shoulder routine could look pretty suspect to a detached observer. Instead of solidarity it suggested, what? Anxiety, perhaps? Fear of humiliation? Either way, he felt his ire begin to rise and did a few squat jumps to diffuse the tension before noticing that the sun was already starting to burn through the mist.

Dave and Hannah were now directly in front of the boathouse, Neil having fallen back a couple of paces.

"I take it you've never done any coxing before?"

"I did some sailing once."

"That's useful."

"No, we capsized," she said, touching his sleeve anxiously. *Nothing phoney about that gesture at least,* thought Perc, still looking on.

"Eights are pretty stable," the coach continued mixing reassurance with realism. "Is that all the kit you have with you?"

She nodded.

"Mind your backs," barked Leonard, as he hoisted his sculling boat off the trestles and above his head. Dave quickly pulled the woman out of harm's way and took off his battered old jacket.

"Here, put this on."

The garment swamped her. "I just feel so…"

She started to giggle as she tried to hitch up the sleeves, "…elegant."

"There should be a pair of gloves in the pocket, and you better have this too," he added, taking the fisherman's hat from his head and plonking it down on hers.

"But what does that leave you?"

"Oh, I'll find something." He returned his attention to the crew who were hovering nearby. "If the rest of you take your places, we'll have Gareth at bow, Sebastian at two, Perc at three, Mike at four, Neil at five, Clive at six, Mark in the seven seat and Steady at stroke."

One by one the crew took their positions alongside the old wooden Simms rowing eight that rested on the racks.

"OK, Hannah, the instructions are *hands on*."

"Hands on," she repeated without understanding, but the crew knew the drill and reached out over the upturned boat anyway.

"*Sliding it out.*"

"Sliding it out," she called and watched as the boat slid out on its runners.

"*Bow side holding, stroke side going under.*"

"Stroke, I mean bow side holding and stroke side going under."

The bow side members of the crew held the boat while those on stroke side darted underneath, grabbed hold of the other side and gave the hull a half turn.

"*Walking it out, mind your riggers,*" continued Dave.

"Walking it out, mind your riggers." And slowly the boat was eased out of the boathouse, lowered to waists and carried down to the water. Leonard, who was fitting the blades into the oar locks of his skulling boat, watched them warily from what he hoped was a safe distance, several yards further along the water's edge. Then, shortly afterwards, Dave approached the aluminium 'silver fish' launch, dressed in the oldest, shabbiest jacket imaginable, and set to work on starting the engine which Perc had attached earlier.

*

As well as learning the pre-outing routines at the clubhouse, Perc was also starting to become familiar with the landmarks along the river. The mile post that marked the 1760 yard mark of the University Boat Race, the old Harrods Furniture depository and Hammersmith Bridge to name but three. Buildings and structures that had acquired a symbolic significance, often beyond that of their original function and purpose as their story, like his, had become part of another much older one. Thanks to his build and recovering fitness, he had been invited to join in with the land training sessions right after he'd arrived in London. Then, after a few times on the indoor tank, Dave had put him in the novice crew and, although aware that 'three' was considered the donkey seat, he had instantly loved the release he got from being on the water. The solo professional athlete had found welcome anonymity with a bunch of amateurs, and the river itself hinted at an answer to Spencer's riddle. These things coupled with his natural self-discipline meant that additional solitary training sessions on a rowing machine were not the ordeal that some of his crew mates found them to be. Consequently, whilst his own technique had improved in leaps and bounds, the crew's balance as a whole was definitely proving to be an issue that morning. An issue that was not being helped by the erratic steering of their coxswain. Perc was intrigued by the way the tension could be felt passing down a boat, as if he was plugged into a larger collective nervous system, and it was at this point that stroke had the inspired idea of beginning to sing. For, just as his position conferred the responsibility for setting the rhythm of each stroke, raising or lowering the rate as required, the personality of the man himself was such that he was equally adept at lifting the crew's mood on occasion as well.

"*When the weather is fine then you know it's the time...*" came the call.

"*... for messing about on the river...*[2]" the rest all chorused in response and, just for a moment, the tension vanished, and the balance improved before another wobble down to bow side threw them all again.

Steady leant forwards, "Gentle corrections, Hannah."

---

2   'Messing About On The River', words and music by Tony Hatch, Dejamus Ltd, (c) 1961. Popularised by Scottish singer Josh MacRae and his 1961 recording.

"But there's something in the water!" the woman gasped in horror.

Glancing over his shoulder, Steady noticed the disconcerting sight of a hand floating by, its fingers pointing delicately upwards through the lingering whisps of mist.

"Easy there," he called, prompting the crew to rest their blades flat on the water and watch as the macabre spectacle passed by. Although closer inspection revealed it to be nothing more sinister than the detached hand of a shop window mannequin, the strangeness of the encounter persisted.

Perc's first thought was of the design embossed on the spine of book he'd found back at the mining town. It had been of King Arthur's sword, Excalibur, emerging from the depths, and seeing those fingers floating by just then almost convinced him that the fabled weapon itself might also be about to make an appearance.

"It's a mermaid!" stroke announced gleefully.

"It's not alive, is it?"

"Hannah wants to know if it's alive," Steady relayed loudly for the crew's benefit.

"Not if it's in this river, it ain't," Gareth shot back from bow.

"There's nothing wrong with Thames water," Mike countered defensively.

"Yeah, and we're all going to win at Henley this year," sniped Neil.

"Anyone would think you worked for them or something," Gareth continued, ignoring the defeatism coming from the 'five' seat.

"As a matter of fact, I do," answered Mike.

"Dreamings," mused Perc silently to himself. "Dreamings."

"There are big boats and wee boats and all kinds of craft
Puffers and keel boats and some with no raft…"

Alerted by the singing, Leonard, who had been paddling up ahead in his single skull, frantically manoeuvred closer to the bank and waited for the novices to pass by. The novices, for their part, were trying to do just that but their boat was approaching Hammersmith Bridge from the wrong position.

"Nearside arch, Hannah," called Dave from the launch.

The boat swerved towards the arch nearest the bank and just made it in time, the blades of bow side catching the stonework as they went underneath.

"In towards the bank now, Hannah, and quickly," came another anxious command from the launch.

Unfortunately, in her anxiety, the cox over corrected, which resulted in the boat heading straight towards an eight full of schoolboys instead.

"Oh my God," she wailed.

Steady glanced round and quickly assessed the situation.

"Watch your blades bow side," he called.

The oarsmen on this side pulled their blades in towards them as they ran alongside the junior crew, their spoons slicing through the air mere inches above hastily ducked heads. Too surprised to say anything, the schoolboys simply watched in amazement as Hannah's crew moved by.

"I'm sorry," she called after them, full of concern, but

when she glanced at stroke he was grinning broadly. "Only schoolboys."

Once they were round the Hammersmith bend the water became quite choppy and, as the boat began to bump, the wind caught the spray from the blades and blew it back at them.

All of a sudden, a large wave washed over them, nearly swamping Hannah in particular.

Genuinely frightened now, she screamed loudly and grabbed hold of the side of the boat for support, her knuckles showing white against the sax boards.

Dave, alert to the rapidly deteriorating situation, pulled alongside.

"Next stroke, easy there."

The crew sat the boat by resting their blades flat on the water while the cox took off her hat and started using it to bail out the water from around her feet.

"How's it going?"

"Can we go home now?" she asked, somewhere between laughter and tears, before wringing her hat out and putting it back on her head. Suddenly becoming aware of the ridiculousness of her actions, the laughter finally won out.

"She's loving every minute of it." stroke grinned again.

"Alright, we'll turn around here," the coach instructed the crew before turning back to the woman shivering in the stern.

"You should find it easier going back, just steer down the middle."

Hannah nodded while he gave the necessary commands. "Stroke side paddling, bow side backing down."

Somehow, they managed to complete the procedure and by the time they passed under the middle arch of the bridge, they were paddling firm again.

"What about that boat?" asked the cox as she peered over stroke's shoulder. Steady glanced round and immediately spotted Leonard coming straight towards them.

"Take a look, sculler!" he shouted.

But Leonard didn't look.

Then it was Dave's turn to holler from the launch, but there was still no response from the veteran who continued paddling straight towards them.

"Hard left, Hannah," urged Steady and the cox gave a tug on the toggle in her left hand. By this time the entire crew had turned round. "*Sculler!*" they all shouted in unison.

Finally, Leonard turned his head, just in time to see the eight directly in front of him. He pulled hard right managing to get his bow out of their way but moving the stern into the eight's path.

There was a loud crunch as the boats collided, the jolt knocking the veteran's cap into the water where it floated gracefully upstream and into Hannah's grasp.

"I'm sorry, I'm really sorry," Hannah repeated over and over as the old man glared at her.

"You stupid bitch, why don't you look where you're going?"

Not knowing what else to say, she was grateful when Gareth replied instead. "Why don't you?"

Steady turned to Dave as he drew alongside in the launch once more. "We all shouted but he didn't hear."

"They're only novices," the coach reminded the old man.

"What?"

Dave sighed before taking up his megaphone. "They're novices!"

"Novices! They're like a bunch of headless chickens!"

"But at least we're free range," stroke retorted, none too quietly.

The rest of the crew couldn't help smiling at this and Dave raised his eyes heavenwards.

"What! What was that?" spluttered the vet.

"He said we'll see what we can arrange... about getting your boat back safely."

But Leonard was not to be pacified so easily.

"Oh no. I'm making my own way back and I'm going to write a full report about this."

The coach shook his head and turned back to the eight. "Okay, whole crew paddling very light. Are you ready, go?"

The crew took a stroke and, as the cox passed, she held out Leonard's dripping cap helpfully. He merely snatched it back from her and slapped it down upon his bald dome.

"Egghead," Steady muttered before resuming his song with the others joining in by degrees.

"*There are boats made from kits that reach you in bits for messing about on the river.*
Or you may like to skull in a fibreglass hull just messing about on the river..."

Once they were safely back into the changing room, Perc turned to Mike who had the adjacent wooden locker to his own, "That thing you were saying about the water?"

Chapter Three

Perc wasn't the only one asking questions just then for, somewhere Down Under, other people were doing the same. Or rather, one person was, and not half so genially either. Fortunately, Spencer was well used to the aggressive interrogation style and could parry shots with the best of them. Besides which, he sure as hell wasn't going to let on about smuggling Perc's passport out to him concealed amongst the rest of his post.

"And you really expect me to believe that?" a skinny young man in a pink polo shirt was yelling.

"Believe what you want, Anthony," grunted Spence as he moved some papers around on his desk. "The fact remains that I don't know where he is."

"I reckon he'd have at least sent you a post card."

"Well, you reckon wrong, don't you?"

The 'office' was cramped, probably because it wasn't really an office at all anymore, just a storeroom for all the extra bits of boxing kit which didn't fit in the gym outside. And worse than being cramped, it was getting incredibly stuffy in there.

Pushed up into the corner of a ground floor space, the only two windows faced inwards and had never been intended for ventilation. They were a leftover from the days when the place had been a garage, ideal for a conscientious foreman keen to keep an eye on the progress of vehicles undergoing repairs, but not great for daylight, air circulation or privacy. Spencer had originally liked the engineering connection and had called the place 'The Machine Shop' accordingly, even going so far as to keep the motto 'We can take them apart and put them together again' stencilled onto one of the breeze block walls. But at that moment he was uncomfortably aware that it was the man in the polo shirt who was set on doing the disassembling and, as he'd also been the one to bank-roll the set-up in the first place, it was probably best to just let him say his piece.

Glancing at all the equipment outside he noticed Lawrence idly hitting a punch bag while he waited for his next driving assignment.

They had each become indentured servants but, for the time being at least, Perc had broken free.

"I could *have* him found; you know that don't you?" Anthony carried on, pacing angrily.

"I know that and so does Perc," grunted the trainer.

"So…?"

"So that's probably the reason why we haven't heard from him."

It was now Anthony's turn to grunt.

"I can't afford to wait any longer. What's the land agent's name in Kalgoorlie? I reckon he might know something."

Spence sighed and shook his head.

Chapter Four

THE ROAR OF RUNNING WATER MADE TALKING difficult.

The sound was amplified still further by the stonework that arched over their heads.

Perc had expected the sewer to be round, but in fact it was an egg shape with the pointy bit lowermost which was exactly where their feet were placed at that moment with gallons of liquid effluent running between them.

And although the lamps on their helmets were adequate to light their immediate path, they could only give scant illumination to the enormity of the structure beyond. But it was enough. Enough for Perc to grasp the boldness of the undertaking and be awed by it. Mike, for his part, was quietly gratified at the effect the spectacle was having on his crew mate. Ever since joining Thames Water as a graduate trainee, he had to endure an endless stream of sewage jokes and even if he couldn't persuade everyone that it was a subject worthy of serious interest, he could tell that Perc, at least, was sold and that Sir Joseph

Bazalgette,[3] the mastermind behind this subterranean labyrinth, had just acquired another fan.

"So, you see," Mike shouted, "once Bazalgette had completed the system there was no more raw sewage flowing into the Thames and no more out-breaks of cholera."

"The bloke's a visionary!" Perc shouted back.

"I doubt he would have called himself one. Engineer, yes, more than that…"

"But to keep an idea this huge in your head for so long…"

"Well, yes, when you put it like that." Mike smiled before looking round for the other people in the group. Perc's head was pounding, and not just from the smell and the thundering water. Mike had explained how, depending on volume of flow, the contents of one sewer could be emptied into other sewers at different levels. Sewers within sewers. Circles within circles, or rather eggs within eggs. Eggs with shells that didn't crack due to the Portland cement Bazalgette had decided on using. A cement that, partly due to the amount of clay in the mixture, became harder and stronger when it came into contact with water. An obvious choice in retrospect though, apparently, one that prior to its deployment in these drainage works, other engineers had been highly doubtful of. It must have taken considerable guts on the part of Bazalgette to use it so

---

3   Sir Joseph Bazalgette, 1819–1891, English Civil Engineer whose most notable achievement was the creation of an integrated and effective sewage system for London. Whilst accounts of his engineering projects are relatively comprehensive, there are sadly all too few descriptions of Sir Joseph the man. For the few clues there are, Stephen Halliday's book: *The Great Stink Of London, Sir Joseph Bazalgette and The Cleansing of The Victorian Metropolis*, Sutton Press, 1999, is invaluable.

extensively on a project so huge, even if he had instigated rigorous testing procedures beforehand. Perc respected guts. Someone willing to climb into the ring against an unknown quantity, test them out with exploratory jabs whilst maintaining his own defence was something he could wholly identify with and from that point on he began to feel a profound connection with this eminent Victorian.

"Of course, he built bridges too," Mike had added conversationally once they were back above ground and freed from the need for shouting and catering to the specialist interests of the other members of the group.

"Which ones?"

"Putney and Hammersmith for a start."

"Our bridges!"

"If you want to think of them like that?" smiled his guide. "Why not check out his bust on the Victoria Embankment sometime?"

"I will."

In fact, Perc had done so immediately afterwards, so keen had he been to find out more about 'Sir Joseph'.

The bronze bust and its marble alcove were close to the river, a position which struck the Australian as being completely appropriate and he was pleased by the face as well. The aristocratic nose, handlebar moustache and impressive mutton chop side whiskers offset by friendly eyes made for a pleasing combination. Gravitas without intimidation.

"Good on yer, mate," Perc heard himself saying out loud.

In the weeks that followed he had made a point of

reading all he could about the engineer, his work, his character – not that there was much to go on there and the challenges the great man had faced. These discoveries and the resulting ruminations they prompted he then shared with Mike during grabbed, post-training chats at the club.

Mike, for his part, sensed that this was the first time his crew mate had ever undertaken a personal research project of this kind and was happy to play the role of undergraduate tutor by suggesting further visits to relevant repositories of municipal plans and drawings.

He almost envied Perc the luxury, he certainly envied him his seemingly relaxed schedule when things seemed to be accelerating at such a pace in his own domestic life. The exchanges he had with the Australian were a reminder of the bigger picture and a welcome bonus to time spent on the water. One day, just as he was looking forward to hearing about Perc's latest discovery, they were summoned into the clubroom by Dave. Quickly gathering up their respective bags of kit, they had made their way through the bar area and into the meeting room beyond. An insignificant shift of location on the face of it, but for some of the veterans it seemed like a defection.

"I say, Dave, that crew of yours isn't safe to be let on the water," Leonard was shouting.

Dave, for his part, was on his hands and knees trying to light the gas fire while Hannah shivered nearby. For, unlike the men, there were no rooms for her to change in let alone anywhere to have a warming post-outing shower. A lone 'Ladies' toilet being the full extent of the facilities available to her. 'Ladies' only ever being allowed as 'guests', and never as members themselves.

"You'd just keep them on the tank, I suppose?"

"On the tank? I'd keep them *in* a bloody tank!" quipped the vet much to the amusement of the cohort clustered around him.

"Very funny," muttered the coach as the flame finally caught.

"Take no notice," he urged the cox before pulling the chair with her sopping wet sweatshirt draped over it closer to the heat. "I'll just get you a tea and then I'll say my piece proper."

"Time for a little chivalry, I think," Mike murmured to Perc, before walking over to the cox. "Well done, I thought you steered really well, this morning."

Hannah, warming to the compliment, whispered back. "Do you really think so? I'm always worried we're going to have another collision."

"You're getting better with every outing."

"How did you manage before? Before I came along, I mean?"

"Either Dave would cox us, occasionally one of the vets or anyone else we could persuade.

"The thing is after one outing, they never wanted to go out with us again!"

"Like a bad date."

"Well, it's not for the fainthearted, I suppose."

"So how often do you come down here?"

"As often as his wife lets him," piped Steady.

The woman smiled but her eyes remained on Mike. "Doesn't she like you rowing?"

"She doesn't know," the stroke man interrupted again before approaching the hearth also. "He keeps telling her he's going out to fetch the milk."

This time it was Mike's turn to smile. "It's a bit like that, she's expecting you see, quite soon now in fact, and we'd like to have it at home, if possible."

"Doorstep delivery, she's insisting on it," confirmed Steady with a cheeky grin and stubbing out his ciggie. Dave eyed the stroke man dubiously before handing the cox her tea and directing Perc to pull the partition door closed.

"Look, I know you've all got other lives, but if you really want to silence the insults from the bar, you're going to have to put in a bit more time and effort."

"What have you got in mind?" asked Gareth.

"The Eight's Head."

"Yes!" exclaimed Neil.

"At last," added Clive.

"What's the Eight's Head?" asked Perc.

"Just the biggest race on the tideway, that's all, usually there's over four hundred crews competing," answered Neil.

"But the beauty of it is," Dave continued more evenly, "that it's against the clock, so even a low placed crew can do well."

"That's my philosophy out of the window then," said stroke, tossing his cigarette packet into the bin.

"You had a philosophy?" bow asked incredulously.

"As the great Sydney Smith[4] once said: '*Take a short*

---

4   Sydney Smith, 1771–1845, English writer, wit and Anglican cleric.

view of the dangerous business of life and look no further than dinner or tea'."

"Who's Sydney Smith?"

"I don't know, that's just what it says on the back of this box of matches," answered Steady. "Speaking of which, I suppose they'd better go the same way as the ciggies, hadn't they?"

"Sydney Smith said something else as well," added Dave, evidently pleased by stroke's symbolic gesture. "*'The meaning of an extraordinary man, is that he is eight men, not one man.'*"

"What's that again?" asked Perc, intrigued.

"Don't encourage him with the motivational quotes," groaned Gareth, "we'll be here for another half hour, at least."

"Consider them pearls of wisdom," urged Steady loftily.

"If I were Dave, I'd just consider them pearls before swine, and be done with it," replied Gareth.

"Thanks a bunch," retorted Hannah.

"He didn't mean you, obviously," interjected Neil hastily.

"You're a pearl already," soothed stroke.

"Thanks, I think," replied the cox, "but I am meant to be a member of the crew too, aren't I?"

"For the benefit of eight men then, eight men *with* small cox," grinned Perc persuasively.

"*'The meaning of an extraordinary man is that he is eight men, not one man,'*" resumed Dave, gratified to have at least one receptive listener, *'that he has as much wit as if he had no sense, and as much sense as if he had no wit;*

that his conduct is as judicious as if he were the dullest of human beings, and his imagination as brilliant as if he were irretrievably ruined."

"Are you going to tell us which one of us matches which characteristic?" asked stroke mischievously.

"No," replied the coach, "I'm just requesting the interested parties to put their names down on this piece of paper and let them find out for themselves."

"Trial by combat," observed Gareth.

"Like knights of old," enthused Perc.

"Oh my God!" wailed Hannah.

Chapter Five

ANTHONY WAS DRIVING HIMSELF THAT DAY. Partly because he was trying to cut down on Lawrence's hours and partly because he wasn't keen on the kid seeing anything which might undermine the image his boss had been striving to cultivate. The Kalgoorlie suburb he'd remembered from his youth hadn't changed much and viewing it again through the windows of the truck reminded him why he had worked so hard to get away from the place. But there were answers here too, maybe, if only he could bring himself to ask the right questions. People who had known Perc and himself when they were youngsters. Perc, the hearty Aussie, and Antonius, the skinny Greek kid with the unruly hair.

He stopped the truck and bought some cigarettes from a corner store. Having taken his money, the guy behind the counter handed over the packet without a word of small talk or any attempt at up-selling to increase the value of the sale. Maybe his English wasn't good. Maybe he was an immigrant too. *Loser*, thought Anthony dismissively as he tore off the cellophane wrapper and lit up. Getting back in the cab, he glanced in the mirror and was taken aback by the pale, haggard face starring back at him. It wouldn't do to make any social calls looking like this. Even he couldn't pull off the 'Successful businessman just back from Perth' routine looking like this. The circles under his eyes would undermine every word he spoke. Besides, his potential audience would soon reason, exactly as Spencer had done, that if he was going around asking questions about Perc's whereabouts then the partnership between them both wasn't so good anymore. And if that partnership wasn't so good anymore, maybe his other businesses interests weren't doing so good either. What was Anthony Mandrakos Enterprises without its local hero?

It was late afternoon now and he didn't fancy the long drive back to the city. He'd have to find a place to stay, but it better not be here, too many people might recognise him. Even though he'd moved his centre of operations to the big city five years ago, he'd been so relentless in his publicity campaigns that he'd met every local radio, TV and press journalist around. Many people would remember him from his time working at the store too. That's where it had all begun really, the sales talk, the patter. He'd always prided himself on being a sharp dresser and had the tongue to match the wardrobe. No fake Ralph Lauren for him, only the best labels would do and, as an employee, he'd got the big discounts to bring them within reach. He knew for a fact he'd been the best sales assistant they'd ever had. Always had the top commission, so it hadn't been long before he'd moved on from selling clothes to selling other things, most of them legal, a few not quite so much, which in turn lead to his involvement in the fight game. Not that Perc or Spence were ever crooked, that's why the set-up had worked so well. They were happy to let Anthony work his side of the street while they had worked theirs. Both gaining something from the other, but it was only latterly that Tony had started to realise he needed them much more than they needed him. Spencer had other fighters and Perc had always been something of a lone wolf and careful with his money. That was another thing, he needed to tell Perc about the money, tell it to him in person, much better to do it that way than for him to find out from someone else, someone like his accountant for instance. It was even possible Perc already suspected his manager of siphoning off part of his share to bankroll other enterprises. Not that he'd always done it, only just recently. And the worst of it was that he'd set up the last fight knowing that Perc might be outclassed. The promotor had wanted a name and although Perc wasn't ready to meet such an experienced opponent Anthony had persuaded him otherwise, effectively feeding his man to the lions. Then, more recklessly still, he had placed a large bet on Perc winning despite, or rather because of, the odds. Initially Perc had been enthusiastic about the match, regarding it as a big step up, but Spencer had known from the start it was a bad move. Bad for them all. Suddenly, the nausea and self-loathing that had been gnawing away at him all day hit Anthony with such force he felt compelled to get away somewhere by himself.

Spinning the truck round, he started heading north and by the time he reached the abandoned mining town it was almost dark.

He kipped in the truck, even though it was parked

right outside his property. He'd never liked roughing it and so any idea of sleeping in one of the old bunk houses the way Perc had done was dismissed out of hand. That said, he wasn't averse to having a poke around inside them in the clear light of day. After all, he might as well see what his money had got him, or rather Perc's money had got him! The place certainly looked different to when he'd first seen it in the slide presentation at the hotel months earlier. On that day the buildings had seemed less dilapidated. Thinking about it again they had been relatively small in the frame with a lot of sky above and a lot more foreground in front.

Mingling with the movers and shakers at the Burswood Island Resort, Anthony had been desperate to be part of the syndicate that was being pitched to him and had quickly signed up for his own parcel of land. It was potential that was being sold, but it was the idea of belonging that had clinched the sale. Maybe they weren't all Rotarians or Freemasons, but they had struck the young manager as being men of substance and, more than that, they had roots. With a piece of real estate like that in his portfolio, he'd feel more rooted himself and the fact that the plots in question had a storied history meant that he'd get a share of that heritage too.

Wiser heads might have decided to travel east and check out the location for themselves first, but Antonius Mandrakos had been too fired up to bother. Not so today.

Like the similarly abandoned Gwalia, the mining town could lay claim to at least some amenities and Lawrence had given him sufficient information to orientate himself. But even though working out where his own holding was in relation to the schoolhouse and the church had been easy, getting the generator going was quite beyond him. Consequently, he decided to wait for sunup before venturing anywhere inside.

At least his plot boasted one of the few buildings that still had a roof, there were some sticks of furniture on the porch and the place seemed watertight. He was also intrigued to find some old newspapers tucked in a corner, brittle but still readable and dated from the 1960s. That was the time when the place had been abandoned to the elements and, coincidentally, the same decade as his birth. Just. A fact that made him a couple of years older than Perc. Beginnings and endings all rolled into one. Along with the papers there was a book with a faded red cover. The gold lettering on the spine had been bleached to almost nothing but, glancing inside, he discovered it to be a copy of *The Boy's King Arthur*. Anthony was just about to throw it aside again when something made him delve a little deeper and, as he began to flick through, he was amazed by the jewel-like colours of the illustrations, which were so at odds with the drab surroundings. Not only that, but he happened upon the name of *Percival* imbedded in the text. Sitting down to read properly, Anthony discovered that it was Percival, alone among Arthur's knights, who had been able to find the holy grail. Perhaps Perc had been reading about his namesake all the time he was out here and had just discarded the volume when he left. But what if he'd left it here deliberately? What if it was a clue?

Chapter Six

"YOU DIDN'T HAVE TO DO THIS," SAID DAVE, addressing the group from the head of the table. They were seated along one wall of an Indian restaurant resplendent with red tassels.

"It's our way of saying thanks," replied Mike.

Despite the polite exchanges, Hannah sensed the lingering sense of disappointment amongst some of those present.

She had told Neil she hadn't wanted to cox the Head of the River race back in February, right after Dave had suggested they put in an entry.

"Can't you find someone else?" she'd asked as they'd made their way back to their respective cars.

"No."

"But what if I screw up?"

"You won't screw up."

"But when the rowing's bad you can all blame each other," she'd persisted, "if the steering's bad you'll all blame me."

"No-one'll blame you. It'll be fun."

"Men are incapable of doing any sport for fun."

Well, she had been both right and wrong about that. Despite her misgivings, she *had* managed to steer an acceptably straight course after all and, more importantly, without any collisions. She was so relieved she'd even been able to laugh about it afterwards. Particularly after she had realised that there were other coxes who were even more inexperienced than she was!

Neil on the other hand had been grumpy ever since. Possibly because she'd shouted at him not to shorten his stroke as they were going under Putney Bridge after the finish. But that was what the cox was supposed to do, wasn't it? Seemed like she was damned if she did and damned if she didn't. At the start, coxing had seemed like a way of confronting her demons, not that she'd ever let on to anyone about her fear of water. Being the sole female in a team of high-powered merchant bankers was not the place to open up about anything that might be considered a weakness. Managing the debt of a small country on the Asia Pacific rim was demanding enough without people doubting her ability to 'hack it'. But the river had challenged her in ways that overly optimistic financial forecasts and disappointing returns never had.

Contemplating 'her' crew for a moment. another realisation struck her, and it was out of her mouth before she'd even realised it.

"You can always tell a bunch of oarsmen because they spend their evenings examining their hands."

"Yeah, it's really disgusting the way they just drop bits of blister everywhere," Steady responded. "Why can't they use the flesh trays provided?"

"How does a flesh tray differ from a flesh pot?" Gareth enquired, passing round the tray of naan bread.

"With one you're red and raw before you go in, and with the other you're red and raw when you come out."

The tray stopped before Neil, who turned up his nose.

"Have some," insisted the bow man.

"I'm not hungry."

"I looked up the word *companions* in the dictionary and it means people who have broken bread together."

"It's from the French word for bread, of course," added Sebastian, patiently resigned to the general lack of knowledge and appreciation of his native language amongst the rest of the crew.

"See, even Professor Jacques Clouseau, I mean Jacques Cousteau, help me somebody, agrees, so you're having some."

"I said I wasn't hungry—"

But before he could say more, Gareth had rammed a piece inside Neil's mouth, adding the words "*C'est bon, oui?*" for emphasis.

"*Non!*" the number five man managed to splutter in reply. "I mean, what are we celebrating here anyway? The only thing we accomplished was giving the veterans a laugh?"

"We're bonding."

"Over going out numbered 420th and coming in 419th! Do me a favour!"

"It doesn't bode well," Clive agreed gloomily.

Stroke glanced at Gareth who was tilting his head from side to side and tugging his ears vigorously. "What is it?"

"I don't know," replied the bow man. "Neil says

something then there's this echo. It happens after every outing on the river."

"Must be reverberation," mused Steady.

The others smiled.

"Ah, hark at the stroke man," Neil shot back, "Everything's always a joke to you, isn't it?"

"Just keeping things on an even keel."

"If you all trained properly you should be able to get into any boat and make it work, irrespective of who's in it." The voice was Dave's as his eyes scanned the faces.

"But it's no good thinking I'm alright and the other guys are all wrong. You've all got to find the balance and adjust your hand heights accordingly, and you've all got to *try* and row together."

Neil snorted but Dave was undeterred and Perc, for one, listened intently as he continued.

"If you can do that *one* thing there's nothing to stop you going for a full season's rowing and, with a bit of luck, by the end of it, maybe you won't even be novices anymore."

"I'll never remember all this technical stuff, I can only remember lines and stage directions," murmured Mark disconsolately.

"What did you make of them all, Hannah?" asked Dave.

"I thought they were going alright," she began cautiously, "until they started to slacken off a bit."

Neil glared at her and fumed silently.

"*Slacken off!*" interjected Steady with mock incredulity.

"Women! They're never satisfied," reflected Gareth.

"You're a natural." Dave beamed at Hannah, before raising his glass. "Here's to Tankards!"

"Pot hunting!" shouted stroke.

"Medals!" shouted bow.

"The grail!" shouted Perc

"And don't bother to gift wrap," added Hannah.

Chapter Seven

IT WAS LATE BY THE TIME ANTHONY GOT BACK TO Perth and it reminded him of the other reason why he had employed a driver. It was because he, Anthony, wasn't much good at it. He had stopped a couple of hours after leaving his grubstake and ordered a breakfast. The toast was like sandpaper and the marmalade could've doubled for Araldite. But the phone worked and he had called Spencer at the gym and told him to expect him after the evening training session. He then called Lawrence at the office and told him the same.

They were both taken aback when he finally staggered in. It wasn't so much the crumpled clothes and the stubble as the hair. Denied its usual assortment of hair products for forty-eight hours, it had reverted to its natural curly state.

"What happened? asked Lawrence, aghast.

"A little business out of town," Anthony fenced as he moved in front of the fan and placed the faded red book on the desk.

"Yeah, well it's been happening in town too. A couple

of guys came round to see you today, said they were betting agents."

"Oh, yes?" the Greek replied, trying to sound casual.

"Yeah," continued the youngster, "quite overstayed their welcome too, snooping around, expecting me to make them coffees. One even asked me to go out and buy him a sandwich!"

Anthony smiled, it was almost like hearing himself at that age. "And did you?"

"Did I f—!" Lawrence checked himself, not on Anthony's account but on Spencer's. He'd never heard the older man blaspheme or cuss and suddenly he felt he would diminish himself further in the trainer's eyes if he did so then.

"Lawrence, would you mind doing something for *me* though?"

"'Course not, Boss. You pay me to do things for you."

"Such loyalty! Well, Lawrence, first thing tomorrow I want you to wash the truck and take it back to the dealers. I then want you to accept their best trade-in offer and ask them to make the cheque out to the two men who called at the office today. I'm sure you took their names anyway, didn't you?"

"Just the way you taught me."

"Good. So, after that I want you to go back to the office and wait for them, because I bet they said they'd be back again tomorrow, didn't they?"

"Yeah, well I was kind of hoping you'd be there to see them yourself next time because I really don't like their attitude."

Spencer had a job not to laugh at the irony of hearing this from the kid, but just about managed to hold it in.

"Well, you just give them that cheque," Anthony continued without missing a beat, "and then you tell them that you're looking for a job, and if they offer you one, I bet you'll start liking them a whole lot better."

The youngster's eyes darted between the two older men, unsure as to whether or not he was having his leg pulled. The fact that Spencer looked almost as surprised as he was convinced him they weren't. "Am I really that obvious?" he asked after a pause.

"Never kid a kidder, particularly one who's better at it than you," replied Anthony proffering a hand.

The youngster hesitated a moment before shaking it quickly and leaving without another word.

Once they'd heard the truck roar away outside, Anthony slumped into a chair and pushed the red book towards Spencer.

"I found this out at the mining town."

Gnarled hands turned the book over, felt the embossed image of Excalibur rising from the waters on the spine and read the faded gold lettering above it.

"*The Boy's King Arthur*, so?"

"It's for kids, well, boys!"

"There's a lot more men who are boys, than boys who are men," Spencer observed drily before pushing the book back towards his visitor.

The comment hit home and, in his travel weary state, Anthony was almost prepared to admit as much. Almost, but not quite. "Did you know Sir Percival was the knight who ended up finding the grail? It seems Lancelot had screwed up too badly to be worthy of claiming the prize."

Spencer shrugged, "Arthur's one of your European legends, isn't it?"

"Northern European."

"Yeah."

"We southern Mediterranean's have *The Iliad* and *The Odyssey*. Ever been to Europe, Spencer?"

Spencer shook his head.

"But if you had the chance, where would you choose?"

"Somewhere with a lot of water."

"Still nothing from Perc?"

Spencer starred at him for a long time before producing a post card from his pocket.

Anthony took in the British stamp and the symbol for running water.

"Would you consider driving me to the airport tomorrow, Spencer?"

"Am *I* still on the payroll?"

Chapter Eight

HANNAH AND THE REST OF THE CREW WATCHED intently from the bank as another crew from their club which included several veterans raced past a second slower crew and won their heat. Their cox, wired up with a small microphone and amplifier, otherwise known as a cox box, had been able to communicate with his crew easily throughout.

"Whatever we do, they'll still have the edge," muttered Steady, uncharacteristically cast down.

"Why?" asked Hannah, just as pained by the spectacle as the rest.

"Faster boat, better blades, cox box..."

"A cox box doesn't make that much of a difference, does it?" asked Mark.

"It does if you're at bow," grumbled Gareth. "We can hardly hear a thing Hannah says."

"Maybe if I gave her some lessons in voice projection?" offered the actor.

"I'm sorry, guys."

"It's not your fault," Steady continued kindly, "it's all

the seniors and those old gits nabbing the best equipment for themselves."

"They're not all bad," Hannah corrected. "Some of the vets I've spoken to are quite friendly."

"It's just that the ones that aren't are the most vocal," observed Gareth.

"*You can't use that boat, you're too crap, use that old tree trunk instead. You can't use those carbon fibre blades, use those old wooden spoons instead.*"

"Are you sure you don't mean teaspoons?" asked Steady, embracing the absurdity.

"Sorry, no. I didn't mean teaspoons at all," the bow man went on, building up a head of steam. "I meant tea *strainers!* Obviously, we should all be using tea strainers with lots of nice little holes in them."

"Just the job to help a struggling crew along," added Neil ironically.

"I hear they have very fancy tea strainers these days," Steady continued. "Stainless steel ones, non-stick, non-drip…"

"Non – *sense!*" Clive chimed. "Great for catching leaves but not the water."

"I wouldn't drink anything made from this filthy stuff anyway," interjected Gareth with a nod and a wink towards Mike. "No matter how many times it had been strained, boiled, or chlorinated."

"There's nothing wrong with Thames water!" Mike protested, unable to resist the bait.

"Only if you've got a shed load of iodine tablets handy," Gareth shot back.

Fortunately for him, Mike then spotted his wife and was able to excuse himself from further ribbing.

"I'll meet you guys back here just before two," he called, loping off to join her.

"And I'll go and get myself weighed for you guys," piped Hannah, "and if I'm not back in half an hour you know I've drowned myself in shame." Perc decided to take advantage of the lunchtime recess by stretching out under one of the horse chestnut trees and glancing up at the sunlight glinting through the leaves. Somewhere a tannoy announcement began to relay information but to Perc just then it was no more than a prelude to a dream. *"The last race before lunch will be the Senior One, Ladies coxed Fours. And, once again, I must apologise to competitors for the late running of races this morning, but we had trouble rounding up the swans on the river."*

Perc's eyes were closed even before the voice had finished and a broad smile spread across his face as his mind become a kaleidoscope of flapping wings and dappled sunlight. Pretty soon it was all rotating gently, pulsing with white, green and gold lights until in the middle of it all a black dot appeared, like the hub of a wheel. Then, in no time at all, this single black dot seemed to have been joined by another and the two dots had become boots, shiny black boots, walking directly towards him. Perc opened his eyes to see who it was, but such was the vibrancy of the surrounding light show, it seemed to take an age for him to discern the outline of a male figure in a very formal grey Victorian suit. And somehow, atop of all this was a face, but the face was the hardest to discern of all because the wearer of the suit was also the possessor of the most impressive set of white whiskers he'd ever seen. Beards he'd been familiar with, but these were *whiskers*, teased and groomed to perfection. They were also, tonally speaking, almost identical to all the swan feathers flapping around the periphery.

Only the eyes shone through and there was something so friendly about them that any sense of anxiety Perc might've felt was immediately banished. "Bloody hell," he exclaimed, leaping up. "Baz! I mean, Sir Joseph! I didn't expect to see you here."

"All things considered I wouldn't have thought it so very surprising."

"It's just that I'm a great admirer of yours."

"Indeed?"

Sir Joseph took in Perc's figure-hugging red Lycra outfit and raised an eyebrow, "I'm sorry, I didn't catch your name, young man."

"Perc, Percival Morgan."

"Ah, Sir Percival, like the knight in the story, eh?" enquired Sir Joseph, taking Perc's hand but still looking somewhat perplexed by his costume.

"No, just plain Percival, you're the only knight round here."

"Hah! So, this apparel is not something to be worn under a suit of armour?" he said it with a smile; at least Perc thought he was smiling, but with that massive moustache he had on him it was virtually impossible to say. But the eyes, there was definitely a twinkle in the eyes.

"You swim perhaps? I seem to remember another athletic fellow a few years back wearing similar attire, same colour too, swam the channel. Webb was the name, Captain Matthew Webb[5]. Got drowned later poor

---

5   Captain Matthew Webb, 1848–1883, became famous after becoming the
     first recorded person to have swum the English Channel. After which, he

chap, trying to swim below Niagara Falls. Reckless, very reckless. Such a volume of water and no way of calculating the undertow."

"The volume of water, that's the thing isn't it?" Perc responded eagerly. "It's the thing that seems to catch people out all the way down the line. Well, down the sewers, at least."

"During the early days of the great drainage project there were certainly several get rich quick schemes that seemed to fall foul because of it."

"Get rich schemes usually do turn out to be pretty shi...shifty, don't they?"

Sir Joseph considered this for a moment, "And might I be right in thinking you have a project of your own and that you are anxious to avoid making such mistakes?"

Perc returned to the tree and indicated that they both might sit beneath it. "If you've got a moment, I'd love to run it by you."

Sir Joseph peered at the grass doubtfully before fastidiously brushing a posterior sized patch with his hand. Watching the performance, Perc produced a splash top from his ruck sack and laid it down as a ground sheet for the old gent to sit on. "Don't worry, it's waterproof," the Aussie grinned. The old gent, for his part, begun to chuckle, and as he eased himself down onto it, the chuckling turned to laughter with which Perc heartily joined in. "Hark at us," gasped Sir Joseph, "laughing like drains!" and the pair of them guffawed even more.

---

went onto perform several other stunts, including the fatal attempt to swim the Niagara River.

*

When Perc opened his eyes again it took him several seconds to orientate himself. That had to be some weird dream, certainly the weirdest he'd had since leaving Oz, and just as intense as the ones he'd experienced at the old mining camp immediately after his last fight.

But there was a kind of unifying theme between dreams, he decided. There he was dreaming about clean water and here he was dreaming about the guy who was a pioneer of modern water purification. Baz reminded him of C.Y. O'Conner[6], famous for building the Gold Fields Water pipeline back home. But whereas Baz had ended his days honoured and respected, O'Conner had topped himself after corruption stories in the press. Strange how you could deal in filth and come out smelling of roses, or else be squeaky clean yet have all the dirt stuck to you anyways. With O'Conner it stuck so hard that the poor bugger hadn't wanted to hang around for the after-show party. It was only later that his name had been cleared. Spencer had said his people had put a curse on O'Conner for his destruction of the limestone bar across the Swan River and that's why he died. He wondered what Spence would make of Baz, hero or villain? Hero surely! He'd love to be a fly on the wall if ever those two got together, and it suddenly occurred to him that his trainer's waterholes connected dreams as well as continents. Time as well as

---

6   Charles Yelverton O'Conner, 1843–1902, Irish born Civil Engineer, best remembered for the two huge projects he undertook in Western Australia: the construction of Freemantle Harbour and the Gold Fields Water Supply Scheme.

space. He glanced down at the grass beside him which looked just as pristine and un-sat upon as one might expect, and before he knew it, he had started drawing a spiral pattern amongst the spikes of grass. He stared at it thoughtfully before getting up and ambling off towards the competitor's enclosure.

Chapter Nine

SEVENTEEN HOURS IS ONE HELL OF A STRETCH for a plane ride and Anthony felt worse than ever after his flight.

He'd flown direct from Perth because he didn't want the added expense of paying for a hotel during a stopover. The turbulence hadn't helped, nor had the airline food, but as he'd paid for it, he figured he might as well try and eat it. Nothing tasted good to him anymore, something to do with the knot in his stomach. Maybe it was a stomach ulcer. Maybe he should start drinking milk. Milk was meant to be good for ulcers. He could try living on oatmeal porridge. Milk and oats, that'd be cheap. Cheap and good. He was going to need cheap and good lodgings too. But he was too much of a realist to know that, beyond breakfast cereals, those two words seldom went together, and certainly not in central London.

Coming up from the tube he grabbed a copy of TNT magazine from a newsstand and found a café to sit in while he tried to get his bearings. From what he read it seemed that most visiting Kiwis and Australians ended up living in West London, but of all the various favoured areas, Putney was closest to the river, and the water was the only guide he had. Certainly, it was the only clue Spencer had been prepared to give him.

But what if the wily old codger had been leading him on the whole time? Getting his own back for the way Anthony had treated him and Perc. He still couldn't figure out why he'd shown him the post card in the first place.

Maybe it wasn't from Perc at all. Maybe Spence had drawn it himself. *"Calm down, calm down. You just gotta calm down."* The waitress was looking at him and he realised his legs were jigging up and down furiously. It had probably been a mistake to give up smoking so quickly, he reflected. Better to cut down gradually, only he hadn't thought it through. Like so many other things. However, as the waitress was pretty and he didn't want to look a complete flamin' Galah,[7] he forced himself to stop fidgeting long enough for her to look away again. But if Spence was out to get him, why had he agreed to drive him to the airport? Was he just anxious to protect his job or did he have another agenda? Spencer always had another agenda, well another way of looking at things at least. Anthony guessed Spencer was wise to the fact that, right now, the gym was the most reliable source of income they both had, so realistically he was unlikely to do anything to spite him. But that wasn't enough to explain why the wily old coot had seemed to soften towards him ever so slightly during that meeting at The Machine Shop. He always had the impression that Spencer had never been very fond of

---

7   Native Australian bird known for flying into windows.

Lawrence either, so would seeing him fired be enough to account for the change? *Nah, doubtful.* To get rid of him as well for a while, then? Nope, as a sports trainer, Spencer didn't subscribe to short term solutions. He believed that all results had to be earned in sweat and hard work and that meant making a long-term commitment. You couldn't kid Spencer with a quick fix. Then he remembered he'd said something along those lines to Lawrence. "You can't kid a kidder," that was it, and Spencer had stared at him for a long time after he'd said it too. Stared at him for longer than he'd ever remembered the trainer staring at him before. Staring in the same way he stared at a fighter when he thought they were ready to learn and might be worthy of serious attention. Could it be he thought Anthony was now ready to learn something too? Maybe he had *already* started to learn something and so was to be rewarded with some valuable information. He chose to believe the latter. He had to believe it, simply couldn't afford not to. After paying for his coffee, he found his way on to the District Line and started heading towards Putney.

Chapter Ten

DAVE WAS REPLACING THE RIGGERS ON THE boat as it sat on trestles outside the boathouse. Then, just as he was turning to pick up his pint glass, he was accosted by Leonard who had a crony named Charlie in tow.

"How far did the novices get?" asked the veteran sculler.

"The semi's."

"What?"

"Semi-final," said the coach, raising his voice unnaturally for Leonard's benefit.

"Huh! It's amazing they got that far!"

"Yes, it is," snapped Dave, slamming his glass down again, "considering what they have to put up with."

"What?"

"You heard. Look!" And with that he pulled a strip of tape off the hull, revealing a deep gash in the shell. "You can't even provide them with a decent boat to race in."

Witnessing both voices and tempers starting to rise, Charlie attempted to play the role of moderator. "Come on, Dave, you know how limited our resources are. There's no other choice than to give preference to the crews most likely to win."

"That's bollocks, Charlie, and you know it," Dave shot back. "The survival of any club is dependent on its members and for a long time now the majority of members at this club have been, what shall I say... well-seasoned. Now, recently, we have had an influx of newer members and if we are to keep them, we need to provide good facilities and good boats too, and that takes money."

"They can have a raffle," expostulated Leonard, but Dave wasn't to be fobbed off so easily.

"Rowing is one of the fastest growing sports and the fastest area within it is women's rowing. Any club that admits women is entitled to grants for equipment and facilities. Good facilities attract good athletes and new blood, and I believe the future of the club should be in the hands of the newer members.

"Over my dead body," shouted Charlie, promptly abandoning his moderate stance.

"Over your dead club," snorted Dave. "Now either you call a meeting and put this to a vote or I'll leave, and you know damn well you won't get anyone else for the money. It's up to you."

The two old men looked at each other silently and then back at Dave.

*

Hannah entered the kitchen followed by Perc. "Do you mind waiting while I have a shower? I won't take long I promise." She smiled.

"No worries, after all, you waited for me while I had mine at the club."

"If things were different there, we could have both showered together." She caught herself. "Not *together, together*, but at the same time. Oh, you know what I meant."

"*Simultaneously?*" He grinned, dumping his bag on the floor.

"That's it. Sometimes, when I'm tired I lose my English."

"Me too! Take all the time you need."

After she had trotted upstairs, he began to look around. Although the layout was pretty swish, the domestic appliances held little interest for him. What really drew his attention were the photos on a pin board, and by the time the faint sound of running water started in the background he was studying them intently. They captured scenes from another life on another side of the world.

Several showed a young girl, was it a younger version of Hannah? Possibly. Unable to decide either way, he wandered over to the patio doors and peered out. Through the gathering gloom he could just discern the outline of numerous water-filled saucepans and so he opened the latch to explore further.

The sound of running water was louder out there and he concluded there must be a down pipe from the bathroom nearby. Stepping carefully amongst the pans, the sound of gurgling water began to mingle with that of wind chimes and distant urban rumble. Lights from the neighbouring buildings alchemised the water in the cooking utensils into pools of liquid mercury and suddenly something dropped into the one right before him. It might have been a gnat or some other insect, but in its death throes it created a series of outwardly radiating ripples. The insect was certainly a fighter, for after a while it seemed to Perc that the circles were welling up from subterranean depths. Each tiny circle rising then expanding outwards towards the perimeter, before being superseded by another.

"What's so fascinating?" She stood in the doorway in a bath robe whilst using another towel to dry her hair.

"Just admiring your collection of saucepans."

"I should've warned you, I'm a terrible cook."

"Ah, is that what it is? I thought you'd set out to make some new kind of water feature."

"No," she laughed sadly.

"There's enough aluminium here to build a spitfire, at any rate." He grinned but she didn't seem to get the joke.

"There's lots of good takeaways nearby."

"Nah, why send out when I can rustle something up," he said following her back inside. "Just point me in the direction of your fridge."

She did and it was virtually empty apart from a bottle of white wine, some eggs, milk and butter.

"Looks like it's scrambled eggs then, and at least the plonk is Aussie."

"Breakfast at this time of night?"

"Sure, best time of day to have it," he replied, placing the ingredients beside the stove. "Gives you a head start in the morning."

She ambled over to the table and watched as he began to search the drawers for utensils.

"I guess it's an Australian thing. You're day when we're still night."

"I don't know," he replied. "Besides, China is only a few hours behind Oz." He opened another drawer before muttering under his breath.

"All the gear and no idea!"

"What?" she asked from behind a curtain of wet fringe.

"Nothing. I was just saying it's a Hannah thing. Nothing in the fridge and the shops have closed."

"I've got out of the habit of expecting company."

He shot her a sideways glance before finally locating his implement of choice.

"No problem. Hey, do you know the egg whisk song?"

"The what?" Her eyes were firmly focussed on him now, the wet hair swept back from her face, a faint smile playing on her lips

He began whisking and inventing his story at the same time. "Yeah, very big about fifty years ago, around the same time as Spitfires, actually."

And then he began to sing, "*We'll beat again, don't know where, don't know when...*"

She laughed, whilst not quite believing.

"*That's* the egg whisk song?"

"Maybe I changed the words a little." He held out the saltshaker and the pepper grinder for her approval and, after she had nodded vigorously in the direction of both, he added them to the mixture and poured it into a frying pan.

"I wish I could remember more old songs." It was said so quietly he almost missed it under all the sizzling. He studied her more closely as he brought some cutlery over to the table and laid two place settings, but she retreated behind the curtain of hair again, ostensibly looking for split ends, and he decided not to press her to elaborate. At least, not just yet. Returning to the stove, he scrambled the egg and pulled two plates out of the oven, burning his fingers in the process.

Pantomiming pain, he wrapped his fingers around the cold wine bottle, uncorked it, brought it over to the table and filled two glasses. She was already sipping hers before he was back at the stove again, tipping the egg onto the plate.

"Got any dead horse?"

"What?"

"Sauce. You know, like tomato ketchup or something?"

She pointed vaguely in the direction of the fridge where, indeed, there was a bottle of ketchup which he then ferried over to the table along with the plates. Positioning the ketchup between them, he watched as she tipped it up and waited for something to appear.

"Here, let me," he offered, taking it from her.

"You shake and shake the ketchup bottle, nothing'll come out and then a lot'll!"

Sure enough, it eventually did, and in a great splurge too, all over the woman's plate.

Perc laughed at the result of his overzealous efforts, but when he looked at Hannah, tears were welling in her eyes.

"Sorry, that's what comes of being ham fisted. Here, have mine instead."

He was just about to swap their plates over when her hand reached out to stop him.

"I love tomato ketchup."

"Then what's the matter?" he asked, sinking back on to his chair.

"My dad used to make me scrambled eggs, but we could never afford any sauce."

Instinctively Perc glanced over to the pin board. "Where is he now?"

She followed his gaze and shook her head from side to side before collecting herself.

"Do you remember the boat people?"

"The Vietnamese boat people trying to get to Thailand?"

She nodded. "Not all the boat people were Vietnamese. Some of us were ethnic Chinese trying to escape persecution from the Vietnamese."

Perc's eyes were drawn to the photos on the board again. "You must have been so young."

"Eleven, and I cried every day."

"Is that what you meant when you said you'd done some sailing once, but you'd capsized?"

She nodded. "My parents had this idea that there would be better opportunities in the West."

"Well, they were right, weren't they? I mean, this place, you're living the dream, right?"

"A series of miracles. There were people willing to help and I felt I must be a very, very eager pupil." There was a loud sniff and then, sweeping hair away from her eyes once more, she looked at him directly. "But, do you know what? Maybe it's not so good if it turns out that the dream, you're living is someone else's."

"High finance isn't all it's cracked up to be?"

"I know it sounds obvious, but the trouble with working on large accounts is they're just so large. Say you're involved in financing a large infrastructure project or something."

Perc tried to imagine it, couldn't, so just listened instead.

"Unless you're very senior, you never get to see the results on the ground. You'll get feedback of course, and the figures, but it's not the same, and before you know it all those feelings of detachment and displacement you had as a child can come back to haunt you, just in a different way."

"Yeah," he conceded after a pause. "Seems like there's always some kind of undertow you need to look out for."

Chapter Eleven

NTHONY OPENED A BLEARY EYE AND TRIED TO make out the time on the bedside clock. Unable to see a thing he then reached up the reading light. The illumination was just enough for him to recognise the position of the hands and to reveal the full hideousness of the room. Nothing matched. He slumped back on his pillow before leaning over to the radio. It was really old and came on really loudly once he'd switched it on. When he tried to turn it down and found he couldn't, he attempted to adjust the large tuning dial to change the station instead, but that wouldn't work either. Then he smelt burning and noticed the reading light had started to smoke, so he turned that off, got out of bed and found the central ceiling light instead. With the radio still blaring he went over to a decrepit TV set and turned it on, causing it to promptly fuse with a little popping sound. After that he ventured into the grime-encrusted bathroom and switched on the shower. However, it was the immersion heater type and had to heat up first and, as it did so, it began to throb like a diesel engine. With the radio assaulting him in one ear and the noise from the shower unit banging in the other, he went to the basin and opened his wash bag, only to discover that several containers had spilt their contents. He looked at the mess, then at his face and then at the tangle of hair on his head and decided that this was a battle he couldn't win.

Downstairs things were no better. The dining room looked like a converted living room, which it probably was, added to which he was the only person in it. That was before a miserable-looking bloke brought him what had to be the worst fry up ever. The bacon was not so much crisp as uncooked ham, the egg had a skin on it that would stick to a wall and the mushrooms were still floating in the brine from the tin. "Enjoy," said the man grimly, and left him to it.

"Penance," groaned Anthony.

When 'the chef' returned to take his plate, he had tried to complain. Complain about the light, the radio, the TV, and the shower as well, but it hadn't accomplished very much. Just the offer of another room, which he knew would be the just same, or the suggestion that he might prefer to move to another establishment. However, the truth was his finances would barely cover what he was getting anyway. It only made the need to find Perc all the more pressing. As he got outside, he felt slightly better. He'd never been fond of walking, but he needed space to think and, as his dingy little room wasn't going to help him in that respect, he started strolling in the direction of the river. Perc, he decided, was one of his three remaining assets. The gym, though not a spectacular generator of income, ticked over nicely under Spencer's shrewd management, but without the draw of its star fighter it was going to revert back to being just another gym and membership numbers would start dropping off quickly. Then there were the mining town plots. If he tried to sell those off now, he'd lose what he'd already paid, or rather all that Perc had unknowingly paid on his behalf. He'd have to hold on and develop them if he was to have a chance of any return at all. But how was he to keep up payments to the syndicate, let alone begin to meet all the additional costs once building work began? He hadn't intended to syphon off a percentage of Perc's income, merely delay paying it into his fighter's account for a while. The line he had planned on feeding to Perc and Spencer was that the promoter had been slow in handing over their share of the gate for that last fight, and hoping they'd go along with it. But that was before Perc had taken a beating. Anthony had reached the water now and he leant over the railing to look at the swirling eddies below. He realised he felt worse about Perc's injuries than about the money and that somehow helped put his financial worries into perspective. Even the knot in his stomach seemed to relax a bit. Turning away from the railing he began walking under the trees and noticed staff of a pub called The Duke's Head tip a crate of empties into a skip by the pavement. Used up, discarded, binned. Fighters had to get up from a knock down if they didn't want to be written off, and entrepreneurs too, for that matter. That was *The What*, but what about *The How?*

What if he found Perc? It might just be that he and Spencer were onto him already, it wouldn't be hard for them to ask a few questions here and there. Maybe he'd get his lights knocked out, it would be a natural enough response in the circumstances. Anthony didn't fancy being punched by Perc, or anyone else for that matter. In fact, that's how they had met.

Antonius Mandrakos, the new kid in school, a weed amongst athletes, had needed protection, and Perc, tall and well-built even then, had been willing to provide it. Why? Out of some old-fashioned idea of fairness and decency? Probably. Perc was unusual like that. Also, possibly, because he recognised in Anthony's knack for fancy patter, something of the boxer's ability of thinking on their feet in order to get out of trouble. It then dawned on him that they had both been seeking out some real or imagined past in order to fix something within themselves. The challenge now was how to fix the fix.

Chapter Twelve

As it was the Sunday following a regatta, there had been no formal training sessions arranged in order that the crew could have a full twenty-four-hour recovery period. For Perc, recovery meant a shortish run round Barnes Pond before a series of weight circuits in the gym. Once he was back in his own room again, he stretched out and reached for the book that lay beside the bed, namely *The Great Stink of London*[8]. It was a volume he had found himself returning to frequently of late, particularly the sections that dealt with his mate Baz. And luckily for him, Baz was at home. Or rather, the reporter for *Cassell's Saturday Journal* had found Sir Joseph to be at home when he'd gone to interview him during the late summer of 1890. But for the Australian, reading the resulting editorial just over a century later, it didn't take much of a leap to cast himself in the role of the interviewer, and in doing so he began to see and hear much more than

---

8   As already noted, this book was published in 1999. However, as our story is set a few years prior to that date the reader should allow that time, particularly when it comes to dreams, can be just as fluid as water.

what was actually on the page. He imagined approaching a substantial but un-ostentatious house in St Mary's, Wimbledon and being shown into the drawing room by a member of the domestic staff, a house maid he assumed. The place was spotless, not a trace of dust anywhere and his nostrils soon alerted him to one of the reasons why, for an aroma of beeswax furniture polish hung in the air. *Now this was what you'd call clean!* He was also struck by the number of photographs dotted around depicting, what he took to be, various family members, their children and grandchildren. No fear of the Bazellgette DNA disappearing anytime soon either, he reflected with some admiration just as the patriarch himself made his entrance. He was smaller than expected, smaller than he had appeared to Perc in his dream the day before, but then Perc had been sitting when the engineer had approached and this time they were both on their feet, facing each other man to man. Perc shot out his hand with such speed that Baz seemed slightly taken aback before reciprocating in a more measured fashion, yet the twinkle in his eye remained for all that.

Because of those eyes and all the facial hair, he appeared almost ageless, however Perc knew that on that August afternoon, Sir Baz was seventy-one years of age and would live less than a year longer. It made this opportunity to speak with him all the more precious and, notebook at the ready, he intended to hang on to every word.

"The warmth of your greeting suggests that we may have met before, but you must excuse me if I don't exactly recall…"

"Yesterday, at the rowing regatta. You were in my dream," blurted Perc, forgetting all pretence of being a journalist.

"Really?" said Sir Joseph. "And what makes you so sure that you weren't in a dream of mine?"

"Well, I, er...'

"I can see I've confused you. Please, sit down, and I'll explain what I mean," said the old gentleman indicating one of the two comfortable chairs close by. He then went over and gave the bell pull a gentle tug before sitting down himself.

"You see, it's part of an engineer's job to think of the future, and of course working as I did on the bridges at Hammersmith and Putney, I became very familiar with you rowing fellows boating so regularly from the clubs there on the embankment."

"Yeah, I can see how that would be the case."

"Good, good," continued Baz, warming to his theme, "So, of course, people being able to enjoy the river and all its amenities was not entirely absent from my mind when considering the effectiveness of various plans and designs, particularly the ones situated in the more westerly stretches."

It was while Perc was considering this that the maid returned bearing a tea tray and, after placing it on an occasional table, she looked at Perc expectantly. With concepts of the fluidity of time and space swirling around his head, dealing with the social niceties of requesting "milk, no sugar", was almost beyond the Australian at that moment but, somehow, he managed. The maid handed him his tea, did the same for Sir Joseph, executed a little curtsey and exited again.

Perc tried to remember the last time he had drunk

out of a cup and saucer and couldn't. Afternoon tea was a ritual long scoffed at but never practised in his corner of the world.

What you had there was a brew, usually left to stew so long you could stand a spoon up in it. Glancing at the fine china, he decided something a little more refined was in the offing and determined to keep a keen eye on his host to see how things were done.

"Now, where was I?" asked Baz, after he had taken a couple of sips.

"Your dream," prompted Perc, praying the porcelain didn't break between his fingers.

"Yes, though really, I think I should use the word endeavour. Certainly with the drainage projects, my endeavour was to apply suggestions, originating in a large measure with others, to the particular wants and features of different districts."

"You're too modest, mate."

Again, the eyes twinkled slightly above the whiskers. "Well, you know what they say about discretion being the better part of valour, eh? But what of *your* dream? You are an engineer also, perhaps?"

"Not even close, mate. If I told you how I earn, *earned* my living, you'd probably have thrown me out in the street for the ruffian I undoubtedly am."

"I rather think not," Baz replied kindly. "Besides such directness is rather refreshing, particularly in one's dotage. Respect is all very well, but too much and one fears they might be dead already!"

"Not you, sir."

"Not quite, at least. Anyway, do carry on."

"Well, like we were saying yesterday, your plan seemed to suffer numerous delays from people who thought they could make their fortune by shipping and selling muck, treated sewage I mean, to farmers as fertiliser."

"Yes."

"Only the proportion of fertiliser to water was so small, none of them could make it pay. There was just too much water for them to move and process."

"Essentially, yes."

"Well, coming from Australia, which is…"

"…one of the driest countries on earth, if I remember correctly," interjected Sir Joseph following his guest's drift with ease.

"Drier than a Pommy's towel, if you'll excuse the expression."

"Seeing as how I'm half French, you're excused."

"Course you are, mate, my apologies, I was forgetting myself in all the excitement of the moment. Well, water is the more valuable commodity for us because of the need for so much irrigation."

"So, surely the simplest idea would be to try and prevent impurities from getting into the water in the first place."

"Keep everything separate from the get-go, as it were?"

"It's by far the easiest, especially if you're not having to deal with centuries of fudging, like we had to, here in London."

"Ah, we have our share of fudgers too, unfortunately."

"I'm sure," Baz concurred with a twinkly smile, "Human nature being what it is, and no doubt many of them came from here to begin with."

"You didn't always send your best, that's for sure."

"No."

For a moment Perc was concerned his frankness had exceeded its welcome yet again, but the old man was merely ruminating.

"But the principle remains the same," he resumed eventually. "No matter where you are, you still have to work with what you've got and lead from the front."

"It would help if a fella had your bearing and temperament, though."

"Bah, it's the nobility of purpose that really matters young man. The rest is just pomp and ceremony."

"The vision, you mean?"

"If you want to call it that. Tennyson expressed it rather well in a poem I came across recently, now if I could just put my finger on it…"

He made to rise from his chair, but Perc, sensing his host starting to tire, bid him to remain seated.

"Send me a message in a bottle sometime."

No, no," chuckled the genial gent. "Your enterprise merits a more elevated response than that."

Chapter Thirteen

ARETH SAT DRUMMING HIS FINGERS ON THE rim of the steering wheel and peered out of the passenger door window at the two black-clad figures across the road. They had just stopped beneath a small second storey window and were almost indiscernible in the gathering gloom, but not completely, and that made him nervous.

The street was narrow, and with cars doubled parked on both sides he had no option but to remain in the middle with his engine idling.

Steady was singing quietly to himself as he considered the best point of entry.

"*Skippers and mates and rowing club eights all messing about on the river...*"

Hannah followed the direction of his gaze and gasped. "You must be joking!"

"You're the only one who can fit," the stroke man whispered back. "Come on, I'll give you a leg up."

He cupped his hands and smiled at her encouragingly before resuming his song once more.

"*With the wind in your face there's no finer place...*"

"But what if we get caught?"

"We won't. Besides it's our club and we're only borrowing a teeny, weeny bit of club equipment."

The woman glanced from him back at the waiting car and shook her head, allowing one solitary word to escape her lips as she did so. "Madness."

"No, Hannah, this is fun."

And despite her protestations to the contrary, she knew she'd hate herself if she drew back now.

All those evenings going through dull financial reports paled in comparison. They were, she realised with a pang, merely the continuation of studious school and university days. Steady was right, this window was her own, uniquely scaled opportunity to reclaim something of that missed girlhood and youth. The adventures they had in the boat were shared experiences, and with the club excluding her from taking to the oars herself, this escapade was hers and her alone. Placing a foot in the stirrup he had made for her, the tingle of excitement was undeniable. Even so, she wasn't about to sell her dignity short if she could help it.

"Just my luck. When I do get asked out, I end up having to climb through a toilet window."

"Some of my most lucid moments have been spent contemplating the porcelain. Just make sure you don't fall into the bowl, okay?"

"What?" she asked, making a lunge for the drainpipe.

"Nothing," Steady replied, darting a glance at Gareth before returning his focus to the night climber beside him.

"Just think about our next race, with everybody in the crew able to hear your voice, responding to your instructions, going for the lift when you give the signal, making the boat sing."

"Urgh. What was that again? The instructions, I mean?" she asked whilst running her fingers along the bottom of the window frame.

"You're late, two, you're *late*," he said, impatience finally creeping into his voice by this point.

"Oh yes, I remember now," came the voice from above. "Steady?"

"What?"

"You are going to be here when I get back aren't you?"

"Course I bloody am." His arms were beginning to shake from supporting her feet so long. "Just get on with it will you?"

"OK," came the little voice from above once more, as she finally transferred her weight from his hands onto her arms and began to climb in.

The relief for Steady was immediate and he was soon singing again. "...*Messing about on the river.*"

She was halfway in now. Halfway in but still halfway out, with both legs horizontal to the road beneath.

"What's taking so long?" Gareth called through the car window.

Steady raised his palms upward by way of response which only made Gareth resume his finger drumming more insistently than ever before, noticing approaching head lights in his rear-view mirror.

He whistled out of the window and, once he had caught Steady's attention, beckoned him back to his vehicle and opened the door in readiness.

"Hannah, we've got to go, but we'll be back, just get

yourself in," Steady called up to the woman before dashing away.

"Don't leave me," came a faint, semi-disembodied voice from above.

"Just get in!"

Whether it was the fear of discovery or the note of desperation that had crept into Steady's normally genial tone, something gave her the impetus to finally pull herself inside. Suddenly the legs vanished and shortly afterwards there was a sad little splosh.

"Uh-oh, amphibious landing," Steady muttered as he reached the car.

Chapter Fourteen

FOUR OF THE CREW HELD THE BOAT TO PREVENT the river carrying it off while the others ran to collect the blades.

"It's like the river's your friend," Mark was saying but Perc was distracted, trying to adjust his footplate.

"Know what I mean, Perc?" he persisted.

"Er, what was that, mate?"

"The river, it might be a bit grumpy sometimes, but it's always there for you, like a good friend."

"Er, yeah. I'd go along with that, shame everything else wasn't as reliable. The butterfly nuts on my foot stretcher won't tighten at all. Anyone got a pair of pliers on them?"

"Here," grinned Mike, handing over a pair.

"Ah, cheers," grinned the Aussie as he got to work.

"They've been set for Neil so long, they've probably corroded" goaded Gareth.

Neil, who was now in Perc's old seat, remained tight-lipped, evidently unhappy about being moved from his customary position.

Once the others had returned with the blades the

crew busied themselves fitting them into their respective oar gates.

Hannah meanwhile was keeping an eye on the other traffic on the river and, after adjusting the small microphone in front of her mouth, she urged the crew to "Push off now."

Her request was met by assorted cries of "not ready" from further down the boat, but she was in no mood for delay. "Ready or not, push off now."

It was a command this time and they somehow managed to move away from the bank in time to allow an incoming crew to glide in and take their place beside the pontoon.

Once they were moving along the stream, the cox made a further adjustment to her microphone before asking, "Can you all hear me?"

"Loud and clear," bellowed Steady from the stroke seat with a pained expression.

"Tell us some jokes," shouted Gareth all the way from bow.

"Try sitting the boat first," she shot back, prompting the crew to look round at each other in surprise.

"Go on. If you can all hear what I say, why don't you do what I say?"

The men quickly moved into the "easy oar" position and watched as she nervously began to stand up.

"Even if you don't want a tankard, I do, so start paying attention." They all looked at her in surprise,

"And that means now!"

There was an outbreak of applause and cheering from an eight nearby and Hannah suddenly realised that it wasn't just her own crew that could hear her. Embarrassed, she promptly sat down again just as an official on the bank turned his loud hailer towards them.

"Halcyon, you have the outside station."

"Oh God," she wailed.

"You'll be fine, just concentrate on the steering," Steady tried to reassure her.

She nodded distractedly. "Whole crew, backstops. Paddling very light. Are you ready? Go."

The two crews slowly manoeuvred into position and the men on the stake boats grabbed hold of their respective sterns. Once they were safely in position the umpire's launch glided up and demonstrated the starting procedure with his flag. "I shall give the commands *are you ready, set, go.* Both crews will leave on the word *go.* If either crew is not ready, the cox shall raise their hand. Are you ready?"

The cox of the rival boat shot up his hand while their bow man took a stroke. While they were straightening up, Halcyon tried to scrutinise their opposition, no easy task as most of them were wearing sunglasses, and then Hannah's arm darted up too.

"Touch her bow."

Gareth took a very gentle half stroke to keep them straight.

"And again," came the command from the cox.

"But, Miss, I'm still sore from last time," came the facetious reply.

No one smiled.

"Come forward," called the umpire and the crews of each boat moved forward on their slides, arms stretched out in front of them, blades buried in the water, legs ready to spring back at the catch.

"Ready, set, go."

There was only a split second between the commands of '*set*' and '*go*' but the Halcyon crew clearly moved away before the opposition. In fact, they had got off to an excellent start and were already half a length ahead. Despite some jeers from the bank, they were not called back by the umpire and so carried on regardless.

"Ten Firm," cried Hannah.

The boat continued to surge forward, the gathering speed disguising their tendency to wobble, and they became vaguely aware of Dave cycling along the bank beside them. "Technique, technique!" he yelled but his efforts to keep up with his crew were soon thwarted when he had to brake for a pedestrian on the tow path.

Despite their early surge, Halcyon's lack of technical mastery was starting to cost them, and the other crew had begun to catch up. Then, suddenly, the opposition began to move out into their lane.

Glancing ahead, Hannah could see that a dog had jumped into the water and was conscious of the rising panic that always followed the sight of living things floundering in water. She knew she mustn't let it take hold; the present reality was too pressing for that, her crew were depending on her. She had to hold onto other things, like the rudder for instance.

With relief came the realisation that the dog was not in any real danger, but that the cox in the rival boat was trying to steer out from the bank to avoid it, the trouble was that she was going to have to do the same in order to avoid a collision, a tactic which would push Halcyon further out into the middle of the river. Their deviation had been so sudden that the bow side blades of the opposition were already over the floats that marked their designated lane and there was a risk of them clashing with the stroke side blades of her own crew. Hannah adjusted her own steering accordingly, but she was still wary of sending them too far out, and the next thing she heard was a groan coming from her own crew. Clive's blade was washing out of the water and the man himself was falling backwards onto Perc's legs.

"Clive!"

Perc continued to row but was all too aware of the distress the number six man was in. Although his eyes had been focussed on the man's back, with his peripheral vision he had been conscious of Clive's attempts to pull his blade inboard and avoid a clash with the ones alongside. Those reduced inches had meant reduced control and the next stroke had washed out early causing the oar handle to catch his crew mate hard in the ribs. Watching Clive crumple brought back the physical sensation of the blow he had taken himself a few months previously. The memory flash was brief but intensely vivid and he felt a rush of nausea even as he grabbed hold of Clive's blade with his right hand whilst trying to keep his own blade moving with his left. With two members of the 'powerhouse' now unable to pull effectively, the boat quickly lost vital momentum and the other crew moved ahead. All Halcyon could do after that was to try and complete the course. Despite being shocked and badly winded, Clive valiantly managed to reach round and grab the end of his blade from Perc before trying to resume paddling, but his strokes were so feeble that Hannah had instructed the bow side members of the crew to lighten their own power to compensate. Somewhere up ahead they heard the sound of a hooter signalling the other crew had crossed the line leaving them to paddle in raggedly several seconds later. Those seconds had seemed like minutes, and no sooner had they reached the finish than Clive had collapsed altogether. Even then, Mike had had the presence of mind to call for three cheers for the winning crew and, somehow, they had responded.

"Three cheers for… hip, hip—"

"Hooray."

"Hip, hip—"

"Hooray."

"Hip, hip—"

"Hooray."

"Enjoy that?" Sebastian asked Gareth.

"Haven't had as much fun since someone tried to bite my ear off in a junior fifteen rugby match," came the dead pan reply.

Dave was waiting for them by the time they had pulled into the bank and running over to Clive, he wrapped an arm around his shoulders before turning to Perc for more information.

"He took quite a whack, may have bust a rib or two," said the Australian.

Dave nodded and directed Mark to undo the injured man's shoes and grab his blade.

Mark did so and other people gathered round to hold the boat and pass the crew their wellingtons and flip flops.

"The rest of you get your own blades out when you can," added Hannah.

As Dave eased Clive onto dry land, the injured man started to tremble.

"He's going into shock, anyone got a splash top or sweatshirt handy?"

Neil reached under his seat and passed a garment forward for the coach to drape around Clive's shoulders, before noticing two paramedics approaching.

"I'll go and get his kit from the car," he volunteered.

"I don't mind going with him in the ambulance, if you want to follow," offered Perc.

"Neil was evidently surprised by the suggestion, prompting Perc to elaborate.

"Moral support. I'm a champion when it comes to sporting injuries."

Grasping the logic at last, Neil headed off under the trees while Dave and the paramedics attended to Clive and the rest of the crew got the boat onto trestles.

"See, Dave, they break in, steal club equipment and still cock things up when they get it."

Dave sighed deeply, looked up and noticed a trio of vets had now joined the circle.

"If you've got a grievance, Leonard, you can raise it at the EGM."

"What?"

"You heard."

"All this talk about allowing women into the club, it's rubbish," blustered Smithy, the second veteran.

"I was going to leave some money to the club in my will, but I won't unless that silly little…" Charlie, the third senior present stopped suddenly as he caught sight of Hannah.

"You were saying?" the cox asked evenly.

"I was saying we'd like an apology, young lady," Charlie resumed, moderating his tone slightly.

"I think we should be the ones apologising to Hannah," this naturally came from Mike.

"You've always been the perfect gentleman, Mike," the cox smiled back at him. "What a pity there aren't more of you around."

Chapter Fifteen

THE X-RAYS PROVIDED GOOD NEWS, SORT OF. Clive hadn't broken any ribs, but he had suffered some severe bruising. Severe enough to keep him out of the boat for a while at any rate.

"Shame your silver shell suit wasn't really armour after all," Perc quipped once they'd found out.

Clive forced a smile as he crept along the hospital corridor with Neil on one side and the Aussie on the other. "I wish rowing boats had indicators and hazard warning lights," the injured man remarked bitterly.

"Maybe you should design some," offered Neil.

Clive snorted.

"You were always coming up with ideas for gadgets when we were at school. Why not now? At least for night use, those bow and stern lights we've got at the moment are useless, especially if you happen to be sideways on."

"That's right," Perc replied. "I reckon it's perfectly okay to be a contributor without being a competitor, it's when you're a competitor without really contributing that the problems start."

Aware that the observation contained a veiled swipe directed at himself, Neil felt another wave of resentment wash over him. Still smarting from being moved out of the 'powerhouse', he didn't see why he should put up with any homilies from a washed-up prize fighter. Yet, if he was being honest, the events of the day had caused him to reconsider his position. Quite literally. At first, when Dave had informed him of the new seating order, he'd thought about approaching one of the senior crews and trying to race with them instead. Occasionally they were known to welcome able, though less experienced, oarsmen into their midst, as it helped lower the overall number of points carried by the boat as a whole. A desirable if slightly devious method of allowing them to compete below their real standard and pick up some easy victories along the way. Neil, with his banking background, merely regarded it as a canny way of hedging one's bets. However, sitting in the number three seat for the first time, he'd been able to not only feel the extra power coming from the middle section of the boat but see it too. From this new position there could be no doubt as to the Australian's fierce commitment nor, more surprisingly, the fact that Clive, inveterate worrier that he was, had gained in strength and confidence from sitting in front of the warrior in the number five seat. And, now that his friend had taken a hit for the crew, he had started to feel a increasing obligation to make a similar commitment of his own.

"I agree," he said at last.

"Always knew you did."

It was such a blatant lie that Neil found himself smiling back before returning his attention to Clive once more.

"And another cox box too! We'll never be able to *borrow* one like we did last time."

"What did you do when it happened to you? Your injury, I mean," Clive asked, turning to Perc.

"Slept a lot, dreamt a lot. Nothing very constructive really."

"I guess it depends on what you were dreaming about."

"Yeah," answered Perc, a faraway look coming into his eyes. "Yeah, I guess it does."

*

Once he'd seen Clive safely to Neil's car, Perc made his own way to the club where he knew Dave would be waiting for a medical update.

He found him on the embankment unloading the boats from the trailer along with Sebastian and Gareth. As he was getting familiar with the routine, he wasted no time in getting stuck in beside them. The boats were actually secured by ties, but they served the same purpose as ropes and kept the craft from sliding around on the aluminium racking when it was in transit. It required a fair bit of climbing to undo the top ones. Once that was done however, and providing you had enough people to help, the shells came off easily and could then be placed on trestles prior to reassembly, a rowing eight being far too long to transport in one piece. The routine invited rumination and reflection. Reflection about the events of the day and rumination about the future.

"I was hoping today's crew might be the one to race at the Upper Thames Regatta," said Dave, unhitching a knot with a degree of force not altogether necessary.

"Where does that one take place?" asked the Aussie, catching the tie as it was thrown down to him.

"Henley."

"Henley? That's a bit *rah-de-rah* for the likes of us, isn't it?" interrupted Gareth.

"The Henley course," corrected Dave. "The organisers leave all the tents up after the Royal Regatta which takes place a few weeks before and then they let the proles in." It was said with a smile and no one was offended. "But seriously, you should try and go to both events if you can," urged the coach. "First, just to experience all the riparian dreaminess of the place, and the second, to participate."

"Riparian?" queried Perc.

"Riverside."

"Ah, riverside dreams, now I'm with you."

"By the way, there was a guy asking about you earlier, didn't leave his name, just said he'd look you up again."

*

All his sparkling notions had taken on a darker hue once he'd heard about the stranger, and although he wasn't exactly nervous, Perc had a sense of unease as he walked home that evening. Instinct was the nose of the mind, both inside the ring and out of it, and by the time he approached Putney Bridge he became certain someone was following him. However, he knew better than to turn round. Besides, there were lots of drinkers nearby, both at The Duke's Head and The Star and Garter and a casual glance would never allow him to scrutinise them all.

However, by the time he was at the junction with the

main road he had determined not to walk home directly. If some stranger was seeking him out at the club house it implied they didn't have his home address, so if that self-same stranger was following him now, Perc sure as hell wasn't going to make their life any easier by leading them to his front door. He was going to lead them to some other front door instead. Maybe even shake them off completely. He therefore determined to turn left and head for Putney Bridge tube station. Once he had begun walking over the bridge, Baz's bridge, he wondered if he'd been mistaken and whether it was just the events of the day that had made him twitchy. The river, so serene and reassuring in the twilight, made it hard to believe anything even remotely sinister could be afoot. But he was mistaken for, as he turned his attention forwards again, he became conscious of a solitary figure in his peripheral vision. The figure was on the opposite side of the road and almost exactly level with him. Deciding to quicken his pace, the figure on the other side of the road did the same. Perc could've upped his pace still further without effort but decided to make a pretence of stopping to make a longer examination of the water instead. It was now mostly a deep grey but still with a few flecks of pink here and there and the lights in Bishops Park were already on. Slowly, deliberately, he played the part of the romantic sightseer, reluctantly tearing themselves away from the picturesque scene before resuming his original direction of travel. Moving his eyes slightly to his right he saw that the lone figure had done the same and was neither ahead nor behind, just exactly level with him as before. He didn't recognise the silhouette at all, but something about the walk seemed familiar. He did a mental run through of all the people in London that he knew and decided the walk was foreign to all of them. Foreign! The only person from abroad that might come looking for him was... No, the shape of the hair was all wrong and he had worked out the guy was carrying a ruck sack, a fact that ruled that particular suspect out entirely. Both figures were now more than halfway across the bridge and Perc had started to think about what happened on the other side. There were steps on the Fulham side leading down from both pavements and connected by an underpass. This meant that any pedestrian could cross to the opposite side of the road without needing to cross both lines of traffic. Either that, or they could just keep straight on at road level. Back on the Putney side, he'd vaguely thought about heading to the tube station, but that would mean using the underpass to the other side of the road.

Of course, he could wait and see if the shadow used the steps on the far side or try and dodge through the traffic up above, but if the other guy hadn't entered the underpass, then they would both end up on the same side of the road together. Another option might be to only pretend to go down the steps, sneaking a peek at his opposite number as he did so and then, if he happened to observe the mystery man descend the far flight, it would allow him a few seconds to dash into the park on his left whilst screened from view. But then, potentially that also opened him up to the risk of being followed into the park with all its shadows. Best then to stay in plain sight and keep heading along Fulham Palace Road until he could change direction more easily. Relieved to have resolved the issue, at least for the time being, Perc decided to check the position of the stranger one more time out of the corner of his eye. But when he did so the stranger had gone. Still walking, the Australian allowed himself a slight quarter turn of the head, but again his gaze failed to reveal anything. There was no way the phantom follower could've vanished completely in that time. Either he had stopped a little further back which would require a full head turn to confirm, or the bugger had identified his blind spot, dashed across to Perc's side of the road and was now directly behind him. Perc hadn't been paying much attention to the traffic up to that point, but something told him then that the bridge had been almost free of vehicles for the last few seconds. His muscles were already tensing when he heard a familiar voice say, quite conversationally, "Mr Morgan, I presume."

Chapter Sixteen

DURING HIS DASH ACROSS THE ROAD, ANTHONY had managed to slip off his ruck sack and was already holding it out in front of him when Perc spun round, left fist primed and flying. The upper cut hit hard and sent the lighter man sprawling onto the pavement, but at least it hadn't made direct contact.

"Glad you haven't let yourself get rusty," gasped the recumbent figure.

Perc glared down at him.

"You know," continued Anthony, getting his breath back, "you really ought to help me up, otherwise some concerned motorist might just think you were assaulting me. *Poor Australian Tourist Felled in Senseless Attack.* I can just see the headlines now."

"That's because you'd write your own copy," growled Perc, who was in no mood to offer any assistance whatsoever.

"Sometimes you have to embellish the truth a little," replied his former colleague as he dusted off the seat of his trousers.

"Distort and manipulate it, you mean."

"I can't blame you for seeing things that way," Anthony continued as he hitched the ruck sack back onto his shoulders. "And to be honest, I was expecting a lot more than just the one punch.

"Don't tempt me."

"I won't, *I wont!*" the slighter man answered, backing away hurriedly. "That's why I originally thought of waiting for you at the club. They seem to have quite strict rules against fisticuffs on the premises, so I thought I'd be safe there."

"Yeah?"

If Perc was growling before, he was positively snarling now, and Anthony backed away even further before continuing.

"I'd tried every other club on the tideway, before I found out you'd become a member of Halcyon. And I was hoping that if your crew had won today everyone might have gone back there for a celebration. The guy at the bar told me that crews generally do, and it would've made it so much easier to coast in amidst all that back slapping and bonhomie."

"In the hope of letting bygones be bygones?"

"Something like that. But when your coach told me you hadn't won after all, I had to think again."

"So, you decided on this bridge?"

Anthony cast a cursory glance at the structure on which they were standing. "A bridge is a bridge is a bridge, right?"

"Wrong."

The glib tone was enough to make Perc want to knock

him down again. But then he figured knocking him down wouldn't alter anything anyway. It would merely be tantamount to another act of disrespect, not just for Baz's bridge but to the man himself. Hadn't that eminent Victorian personally reminded him that discretion was the better part of valour?

"There's a pub just up ahead," he heard himself muttering between gritted teeth. "You can say your piece in there. Besides, seeing as how you like to think there's safety in numbers, there might even be some other customers loitering around. Though personally, I wouldn't set too much store by that if I were you!"

Fortunately for Anthony there were, and they appeared to be playing a game of Jenga with outsized wooden blocks. A man was about to place another block on top of the Jenga tower but hesitated as the duo passed by.

It seemed like it might topple of its own accord such was the rush of air generated by the doors as they swung violently back and forth on their hinges.

"What can I get you?" asked the smaller man once they were by the bar.

"Guinness," growled Perc.

"Anything to go with it? A bag of peanuts maybe? I know how aggressive you can get when you're hungry."

Perc glared.

"*Two* bags of peanuts? OK, OK. Just a pint of Guinness and er, er…"

He turned and stared blankly at the array of beers. He'd never been fond of the stuff himself but suddenly felt the old urge to fit in.

"Got any local beers?"

"We've got Fullers, that's brewed just up the river," answered the barman pointing to one of the taps.

"Alright, and a pint of that then."

The barman nodded, totalled it up and took the cash.

Anthony could feel Perc's eyes burning into him the whole time, making him feel as if every note and coin that he was handing over had been stolen directly from his fellow countryman's pocket.

"The Guinness will take a minute, so if you want to sit down, I'll bring your drinks over to you."

"Do you want to sit down?"

Perc shrugged and wandered over to a table near the Jenga game.

"Thanks, we'll be over there," Anthony confirmed to the barman who watched the receding figures thoughtfully as he filled their glasses.

"Do you come here a lot?" Anthony asked, sinking awkwardly into a chair.

"Never."

"So, it's a first for both of us."

"First and last, I hope," glowered Perc before glancing over towards the barman. He wished he'd ordered a shot instead. A shot would've been quicker to pour and faster to swallow. With a shot he would've been out of there already and not hanging around with the little parasite opposite.

Anthony shuffled in his chair before bringing the fingertips of both hands together until they were touching. They formed a glass-sized void. When you had a glass in your hand you could fill the awkward pauses by sipping. A glass seemed to legitimise silences. Two hands touching the way his were now, with no glass in between them, made him feel like a supplicant. Like one of those sad saps begging for forgiveness in the Renaissance paintings they'd been shown at school.

Of course, Perc hadn't taken art at school, it wasn't one of his chosen subjects. It clashed with games.

And yet an alliance had been formed based on mutual ambition and respect.

Suddenly, Anthony reached into his ruck sack and produced *The Boy's King Arthur* and placed it on the table.

"If that's the case, why did you leave this for me to find?"

Despite himself, Perc was momentarily thrown by the sight of the faded red cover.

"I didn't leave it for you, I just couldn't carry it."

It was at that moment that their drinks arrived, prompting Perc to snatch up the volume and make room for the glasses.

Anthony took a sip whilst keeping both eyes fixed on the fighter. The Fullers London Pride was not to his liking, but he wasn't going to let on.

After flicking through the pages for a few moments, Perc looked up.

"Ever wonder about the person that owned this book before? Just some kid, probably, stuck out there in the middle of nowhere, maybe dreaming big dreams, like you and I did when we were that age. Ever wonder what happened to that kid? Ever wonder if they got to achieve something, or if they had the rug pulled out from under them, like so many others?"

"Champions get back in the ring, Perc."

Perc clenched his jaw and resumed his page turning.

"And if you were to take just a couple more fights that would be enough to get everything back on track."

"I'm not getting back into the ring," the taller man answered carefully without looking up.

"Neither for you, nor for anyone else. And threatening me with lawyers or making empty promises isn't going to change things."

"It might do for Spencer?"

"Spencer understands."

"Not *every*thing."

The dark eyes finally lifted from the book and fixed on the man opposite.

"I had to put up the lease on the gym as security for a bank loan."

"Say that again?"

If it had been hard to say the first time, it was even harder the second but, after coming this far, Anthony figured there was no point in holding back.

"It was the only bit of useful collateral I still had in my portfolio. The mortgage on the apartment is in both Bianca's name and mine, so they wouldn't accept it."

"So, you put an old man's livelihood and his pension at risk instead?"

"Nobody need end up on the street," Anthony persisted in strained tones, "just so long as I can service the debt and keep the bookies at bay."

Perc slammed the book shut with such force that a fine stream of dust fell onto the table.

It was orange-red, mining town earth and for Anthony it felt like the last grains of hope draining away.

Perc then rose silently from his chair, grabbed the book and strode out the same way he had strode in. Seconds after the door had whipped back behind him, the Jenga tower collapsed.

Chapter Seventeen

THE MEN IN SUITS HAD THEIR BACKS TO THE windows of Spencer's office, but while the trainer faced them, he scrupulously avoided making eye contact. He accomplished this mostly by looking past their shoulders towards the car parked outside. It was shiny and expensive. Not the kind of vehicle that normally pulled up outside his establishment. Every day they had come and every day he told them the same thing, three words at a time, like combination punches: "I don't know. Haven't seen him. He's away maybe." Always the same three sentences, sometimes arranged in different orders, but delivered with such force and fury, they had accepted them as true. But then, that morning, the phone had rung and picking it up he had heard the operator asking if he'd accept a reverse charge call from the UK. The trouble was the two men had heard it too, and snatching the phone from him, they had both shouted the affirmative into the receiver. Spencer stared past them once more, straight into the eyes of the driver waiting in their car. To Lawrence, even from that distance, it was like the old man's eyes were boring into his soul and, biting his lip, he rolled up the dark window and looked through the windscreen instead where, high up, a plane was making an arc across the sky.

*

Perc tore his eyes away from a vapour trail and looked at his companions. In any other context Sebastian, in his loud pink striped jacket, would've stuck out like a sore thumb, but amongst this Henley crowd he fitted right in.

Besides, being French, he was allowed a bit more leeway when it came to sartorial matters. Even Gareth had exchanged his customary striped rugby shirt for a pressed white one and Perc himself had borrowed a jacket for the occasion. The three of them were sprawled on the grass near the start of the course, just opposite Temple Island.

"This is what everyone dreams of, isn't it?" the Australian mused out loud.

"Journey's end for rowers," agreed Sebastian.

"Endings *and* beginnings," observed Gareth. "Like salmon making their way back to the spawning grounds," he added with a knowing wink at his companion's jacket.

"You're just envious because you don't have the courage to wear such bright colours."

"No. I mean it's fine," deliberated the bow man. "Just as long as you don't mind being mistaken for a packet of salmon fillets!"

"A chunky tweed's more your style, isn't it, Gareth?" Perc teased gently.

"I must admit I might be partial to a bit of tweed."

"Brown!" snorted Sebastian derisively.

"More of a nice olive green actually, like a pike."

"A pike?

"A fish."

"Ah, you mean *le Brochet*. And is it a good swimmer too, this pike?"

"Fastest fish in the river. That's why it's called a *motor* pike!" the bow man shot back with a grin.

"Different fish, same destination," reflected Perc. "What's the French word for quest?"

"*La quête*."

"To *la quête*," they all repeated, clinking beer bottles.

And it was indeed the riparian dream Dave had described, only Perc felt something was wrong. Reality had impinged on it in the form of Anthony. Not that his fellow Australian was with them at that moment, but he was somewhere around. Admittedly he looked less wild than he had on that first meeting on Putney Bridge, but it was hard to believe any change was more than skin deep. Since then, he'd followed Perc's lead and got himself a temping job in an office. Being an employee must've grated, but it had financed the haircut and an expanded wardrobe that now included the white chinos, deck shoes and jacket of sombre hue in which he had wandered off in shortly after their arrival at the hallowed rowing course. However, just knowing Anthony was nearby brought his own prize fighting past closer as well, and any notions he'd harboured of creating clear water between them were greatly diminished. And yet, even then, the enormous life size chess pieces on the island nearby were pure Lewis Carrol and another race was about to start.

Not being interested in watching the rowing, Anthony had decided to explore the location and been struck by the way the organisers had arranged it so that the wet-bobs, he was picking up the terminology, were mostly on the Remenham side of the river, and the corporate hospitality tents were all on the other. Pure sport on one bank and pure profit on the other, with the river running in-between. He had wandered over the bridge and standing in the middle of it he couldn't help but compare and contrast the two. It was like old Father Thames, whose face was carved into the keystone directly beneath him, had arranged an object lesson for his benefit. Maybe this was why Spencer had given him the heads up about Perc's whereabouts. He'd always suspected the trainer of having hidden depths and, even though he'd never deemed to share his most personal musings when Anthony had been around, looking down at the water just then, he suspected that when it came to the big stuff, the trainer would possibly favour the oblique approach.

'The answer's there but you're going to have to work it out yourself' kind of thing.

*

Inside the stands, Hannah gave Steady a hard shove just as the tannoy voice announced the latest result.

"I can't believe you missed it all."

"Who won?" asked the stroke man, waking up with a start.

"We did, I mean the GB team did."

"Oh well, that's alright then. Can we have a drink now?" he asked, rising to his feet unsteadily.

"Don't you think you've had enough? It's not even lunch time yet."

But he was already moving away from her. "If we go now, we'll beat the queue in the bar tent."

Although she was reluctant to follow him, follow she did. After all, he had managed to wangle a couple of tickets for the Steward's Enclosure and invited her along as his guest. Besides which, the views from the stands were by far the best for watching the final stretches of the course.

However, as they were making their way through the mass of blazers, hats and long dresses, she was taken aback to see Neil and a woman she assumed must be his wife. The crush made the idea of turning back impossible so there was nothing for it but to press on regardless.

"Hi," she called out lightly.

"Hi," he called back.

"Copious felicitations," added Steady, who was none too steady by that point.

Neil turned to his companion and attempted to make a formal introduction. "Helen, I'd like you to meet Hannah and…I'm sorry, I've forgotten your real name…"

"Just call me Steady, 'cos I'm the rhythm man," slurred Steady.

Helen extended a limp hand to each.

"Yes, you were all in that race, weren't you? The Eight's something or other."

"Head," Hannah corrected helpfully.

"Did you see us?" asked Steady, trying to focus.

"No, I just remember Neil going on and on about it afterwards."

"Helen isn't really into rowing, are you, darling?" Neil offered uncomfortably. "We're only here today because she wanted to see all the dresses and the hats."

"It just seems so silly to me," his wife continued languidly. "I mean, none of you can even see where you're going, can you?"

"That's my job," Hannah explained pointedly.

"And then to finish only one place higher than the one you entered in."

The scorn in her voice was enough to penetrate even Steady's stupor and he began wagging a finger under Neil's nose.

"Glass half empty, as usual?"

"Yeah, I know," the accused man replied awkwardly. "I was blaming everyone else for not having enough skin in the game when it was really me who was coasting."

"To hear you then, anyone would think you were having a nervous breakdown," the wife continued dismissively.

"Maybe I was. I was way too uptight about things back then, that's for sure."

The comment was so uncharacteristic and delivered so modestly that all four fell silent for a full second before Steady spoke.

"Is this a private game of true confessions, or can anyone play?"

"If the river tends towards more transparency in its upper reaches, why can't I?"

"Why not indeed?" conceded Steady.

"Do *you* understand what they're on about?" Helen asked, turning towards Hannah.

"I'm starting to," the cox replied with a sympathetic smile that was more for her husband's benefit than hers.

The wife merely sighed and shook her head. "I knew I should have gone to watch the tennis with my sister instead."

"Thames et Veritas!" pronounced Steady, reaching the front of the queue and raising a glass of Pimm's aloft before toppling backwards into a passing waiter, sending both him and his tray flying.

Startled by the subsequent crash everyone turned round. In other places a cheer might have gone up at this point, but not there and not then. A few yards away Dave merely shook his head and walked away.

Chapter Eighteen

PERC ENTERED THE CLUBROOM AND TOOK IN ALL the activity going on around him. A large trestle table was being positioned at the end of the club room while other members were busy setting out chairs and placing photocopied agendas onto each and, cutting through it all, the agitated tones of Anthony speaking into the pay phone nearby. Somehow, hearing non-rowing business discussed in those surroundings was particularly jarring, and the colourful phrases his erstwhile colleague used from time to time only made it worse. The disconnect hadn't been too bad at first but now, as the room began to fill, he wished Anthony further way than ever. Many of the members were dressed in suits and ties, indicating that they had come straight from work which only added to the sense of formality and serious portent of what was to follow. Yet still Anthony ranted on. Apparently, the payphone at his digs was out of order and, as a temp, making personal calls from the office was strictly forbidden. However, when Perc's suggestion of using any of the other phone boxes in the vicinity had fallen on deaf ears, he realised calling from Halcyon was a deliberate ploy on Anthony's part to make him feel uncomfortable. He was meant to hear what was being said, and if other people did as well, so much the better. It was a none too subtle way of making his former client feel guilty, which was ironic to say the least. Were it not for that no-fighting on club premises rule...

Perc tried to blot out the sound and wandered over to the row of seats where the other novices had started to assemble. They had begun to get used to their crew mate's mouthy associate, but that didn't mean they liked him any better than Perc did. However, they kept their views to themselves and Anthony, for his part, never intruded into their conversations directly. He just seemed to be increasingly around in the background, like the proverbial bad smell. That bad smell was, in fact, an expensive brand of aftershave, but that only made them dislike him more! Perc was relieved when someone began to pull across the sliding doors that separated the bar area from the clubroom, a clear indication that the meeting was about to begin. Deprived of his audience, Anthony wound up his call and moved to the bar area on the other side of the partition. With the doors shut behind him, he found himself alone and his self-perceived outsider status returned in full force. Even the faces in the numerous crew photos seemed to be looking down on him with disdain. However, he found that by leaning back in his chair he could rest his head against one of the doors and still hear what was being said on the other side.

"The whole attraction of a club like ours is that women *aren't* allowed!" someone was saying.

"Here, here," added Charlie from one of the seats nearby.

It was at this point that Steady's hand shot up and caught the chairman's attention. From his position at the centre of the long table, he nodded and gave the stroke man the floor.

"Speaking as a novice, and as a younger member of the club," he began, "I can say that the social element of the club is at least equally important as the sporting side."

This was met by a general chorus of *here, here's* from around the room.

"Many of us come here several nights a week..."

"Yes, to break in," interrupted Smithy from another part of the room.

"We come here straight from work," continued the stroke man unabashed, "we train hard and by the time we go home it's late. There isn't time to meet any women."

"What do you want to meet women for?" Smithy interrupted again.

"Sex!" shouted another voice, provoking chuckles and jeers in equal measure.

"Alright, alright," said the chairman, calling everyone to order before another hand shot up.

"Surely the real reason Dave is so enthusiastic about the proposal is because his architectural firm will get to draw up the plans for the new women's changing room?"

This comment was greeted with general jeering but not from the novices who, all seated together in a row near the back, had subconsciously kept to their order in the boat.

"I'd give you a good deal," Dave shouted back from his side of the room.

"Oh, stick to the issue," Gareth muttered under his breath.

"That would be a topic for debate at another meeting if the proposal is passed," said the chairman as if in direct response to the grumblings of the bow man.

The polarised nature of the debate was causing Perc's temper to fray too, only he was trying hard not to let it show. What a contrast this was from the light-hearted banter he and his crew had shared in that very same room back in the spring.

Hannah had just started coxing them then and everything was bonza[9]. OK, maybe not everything, but he'd been too immersed in his dream to bother about anything that wasn't. Man, how he hated the way politics got mixed up with sport! No matter where you went there just didn't seem to be any getting away from it. How would his mate Baz have handled the present circumstances he wondered? Getting all those London districts on side for the Great Drainage Project must have taken some doing. Bet there'd been a few awkward buggers amongst that lot as well. What had the old gent said when he'd asked him about it? Oh, yeah, *discretion is the better part of valour,* like he wasn't giving away any trade secrets. But of course, *that was* the secret! Strewth! If Baz wasn't Sydney Smith's 'extraordinary man' to his boots.

And before he'd realised it, his own hand had gone up. A fact which caused concern amongst several of his crew mates.

"Quick, feed our monster!" hissed Steady, prompting

---

9   Australian slang for first rate or excellent.

the rest of the novices to search their pockets for anything edible.

"A Mars a day helps you work rest and play to the gallery," exclaimed Mark in triumph, before passing the confectionery along.

The Australian nodded his gratitude and was just about to rip off the wrapper when he became aware of the chairman's voice.

"The person on the back row."

"You're on, baby," muttered Gareth.

Thrusting the Mars bar aside, Perc rose to his feet.

"Don't shoot me for what I'm about to say," he began awkwardly whilst his crew mates held their collective breath.

"We Australians are a bit touchy about becoming gun fodder for your wars!"

Was he joking or being serious? Either way, he had everyone's attention now.

"But believe it or not, both myself and the rest of the novices are full of admiration for the achievements of the older members…"

"Even if they *are* deaf," interrupted Steady none to helpfully.

"Especially all the trophies that are dotted around this room," Perc resumed in what he hoped was a suitably conciliatory tone, "and we want that tradition of excellence to continue, but how can something endure, let alone prosper, if it's also meanspirited? And I ask this as someone with a reputation for being professionally mean."

Although it hadn't been intended as a rhetorical question the room took it as such and, with no response forthcoming, Perc found himself forced to push his public speaking skills further than he would have wished. How did the rest of that Smith quote go again? "*...has as much wit as if he had no sense, and as much sense as if he had no wit...*"

"What I've learned since I got here, am still learning in fact," he began again, "is that great men have the capacity to act outside the confines of self-interest for the greater good. N*oblis oblige,* I think you call it."

The novices cheered at this and several of the other more thoughtful members also murmured their approval.

"Now he's just showing off," Smithy cut in.

"Where'd you learn that then, the House of Lords?"

"No, but it *was* along the corridors of power," Perc grinned back, finding his flow at last.

"Eh?" Leonard shouted.

"He means the sewers," Mike explained helpfully.

This was met with even more jeers and the chairman was forced to call for quiet once more.

It was during those seconds that Anthony, still listening through the gap in the door, finally realised that the dynamic between manager and fighter had changed irreversibly. His idea that theirs was a partnership between brain and brawn had been, he saw now, not only inaccurate, but patronising too.

A form of lazy mental shorthand that had blinded him to the fact that Percy "No Mercy" Morgan had moved up not just one division but several.

"You see," Perc resumed with growing confidence, "fortunately for us, the chief engineer of the Victorian sewer system went further than the specifications of the time required. Way further! Even down to the quality of the mortar."

"With your point being…?" interrupted another baffled veteran.

"Club rules are like mortar! If the mixture's wrong or if it gets too old and brittle, the bricks are going to start crashing down. And were that to happen here at Halcyon it would be like, I don't know…like the end of Camelot, or something. At least for this ocker."[10]

The Arthurian allusion combined with ardent manner of its conjuring took many by surprise, including Perc himself. And whilst a few might have been inclined to scoff at it, the undoubted sincerity of the speaker persuaded most not to. For, truth be told, the young Australian's words had re-awakened the sense of romance which many there that night associated with their sport, particularly in their own younger days, but would have never been able to articulate. Something about the age-old activity of moving a boat by oars made it very easy to feel an affinity with those who had gone before and so, accepting that the boundaries between sport and chivalry might overlap, was no great leap at all. And, as numerous minds reflected on these matters, the room became quieter, allowing Perc to take his seat to surprisingly appreciative applause.

Dave, picking up on the palpable shift of mood, held his arm aloft until the chairman gave him the floor once more.

"So, there it is gentlemen. Bold knightly deeds or

---

10   Uncouth Australian man.

narrow-minded knavery. I know which path I'd rather take, and I'm sure that in your hearts, you do too."

Again, the room remained thoughtful and subdued.

A chair leg scraped against the wooden floor as the chairman got to his feet. Surveying the room and finding no other hands aloft he cleared his throat. "Can I take it we are ready to vote now?"

As he was answered by assorted shouts of "yes" and "get on with it" from the floor he decided to press on.

"Right, we'll have a show of hands. Those in favour of the principle of admitting women members to this club please raise your hands and keep them aloft so we can count them."

At this, all the novices raised their arms and looked round to see who else had joined them whilst the chairman continued counting.

"Is your hand up or down?" the chairman asked, suddenly singling out an older member.

"Er, up," stammered the veteran.

"Right, then keep it up where we can see it properly."

Once the final figure was reached a number was scribbled on a piece of paper and shown to two other men at the head table to check against their own tallies. After getting the nod from them the chairman cleared his throat again and announced, "Gentlemen, the motion has been carried." Then, casting a glance in Perc's direction, he added as a friendly aside, "A result which, I'm sure, will come as a great relief to anyone of us who has ever ventured down a sewer!"

Chapter Nineteen

IMMEDIATELY AFTER THE RESULT HAD BEEN announced the room burst into loud, lively conversation. Congratulations and commiserations, goading and gloating all flew back and forth at once. Dave made his way through the hub-bub to share a word or two with the novices who were talking amongst themselves. "Quite a momentous moment," he beamed. "I have to say, I didnae think we'd break the old guard on the first go."

"You can't hold back the tide," grinned Perc.

"Now it's just a question of spreading the word to the world outside," said Gareth.

"A signal," added Steady.

"*Our* signal," said Clive, wincing a little as he lifted a ruck sack up onto his knees, "but you'll need someone to sit in my seat."

Steady's gaze homed in on Clive. "Only if you don't feel up to it?"

Clive was evidently tempted.

"It'd only to be to Hammersmith Bridge and back, right?"

"That's right. No heavy work at all really," continued Steady at his most charmingly persuasive. "In fact, we could even paddle in fours if you preferred."

The smile on the other man's face was answer enough.

"Good. We aim to be on the water in fifteen minutes."

And with that they made their way through the throng that was now surging towards the bar, but, even in this melee, Perc could still make out the solitary figure of Anthony. Waiting and watching.

*

Truth be told, it took more like thirty minutes to get on the water as, in addition to the stern and bow lights normally required for night rowing, Clive had needed to clamp an extra light bulb to each blade. That done he'd then directed the others to tape a length of wire up along each of their oar handles to link them with tiny magnetic battery packs near each oar gate. Anthony hovered around on the side lines while all this was going on, shifting his weight from one foot to the other. However, Perc was part of a crew now and the sooner his former manager, he was sure about the *former* bit, understood that the better. The crew had made a decision to go out for a paddle and that was that. Being part of a group, and a group of amateurs to boot, was almost the perfect way to mess with Anthony's head. If he took on one of them, he'd have to take on all of them, and any talk of money was utterly pointless in this present company. Besides, anything which might curtail his involvement in *La quête* was inconceivable to Perc at that moment. The knowledge that Spencer's gym had become the latest pawn in Anthony's game only served to make it more compelling rather than less. Fair means had to be seen to win over foul, not just for his sake, but for his old trainer's sake too. What such a pursuit might mean in practical terms he couldn't say. But, in the wake of the meeting, he was aware of a growing sense of confidence and belief. In fact, so secure did he feel at that moment, that he threw out a conciliatory comment. "You can follow us on the tow path, if you like."

"Are there any streetlights along there?"

"No."

"But I might trip and break an ankle."

Perc had a job not to smile at the prospect but made no suggestions.

That was left for Gareth to do. "Why stop with just an ankle?" he growled none too kindly.

An expletive was right on the tip of Anthony's tongue, but a glance at the burly bow man was enough to put him off using it.

Well, if he couldn't beat them, he would just have to join them, that was all.

"And these were new shoes," he muttered plaintively under his breath.

Perc just had time to catch sight of the crocodile skin loafers before Dave called everyone's attention back to the task in hand.

Out on the river, the crew discovered the water to be smooth as glass and one by one all land-locked preoccupations slipped away as they glided along its surface. "Ideal conditions," Dave said aloud. Knowing it would take Clive a while to get back into the swing of things, he got the crew to go through some exercises instead of ordering them a to do 'a piece' right away. First off was a spell of rowing with eyes closed and, with just their hearing to guide them, each man strained to drop his blade in the water as one with the rest of the crew. The still of the evening, the flatness of the water and the absence of sight heightened their other senses to a remarkable degree, and within a few strokes they were managing the trick admirably.

Anthony might just as well of had his eyes closed for all that he could see. Stumbling along the track beside the river, he frequently lost his balance or walked into a low hanging tree branch prompting a constant stream of expletives. But even though he couldn't see where he was going, the decisive, rhythmic knock of the blades as they rotated in the oar gates, kept him orientated.

"How are you feeling, Clive? Dave shouted from the cox's seat.

"Alright."

"Alright enough to try a practice start?"

"Yeah, okay," came the response from the number six seat.

So, Dave made them do a series of practice starts; three three-quarter length strokes, lengthening out to ten full-length strokes, then sitting in the easy oar position with all blades off the water, a true test of their balance as a crew and the extent of Clive's recovery. Again, the results surprised them and, gliding between the resulting avenue of perfectly spaced rippling concentric puddles, each man felt a sense of growing mastery, and their spirits rose accordingly. Maybe it was just the night or maybe it was the fact that they were all together in the boat again, but somehow, there was magic in the air.

*

Meanwhile Hannah, waiting on Hammersmith Bridge as instructed, felt it too. Irrespective of how the vote had gone that evening, she was aware of a shift and that her great abiding terror of water had been replaced by something else. A wary kind of respect and, whisper it, an affection too.

*

Back on the riverside path, Anthony was feeling no such thing. Once the crew had begun its series of rowing starts, he'd felt compelled to do something he hated even more than walking, and that was to break into a jog, and now that his heart was pounding and his lungs heaving fit to burst, the road bridge up ahead with its promise of streetlamps and pavements offered the only salvation in sight. However, the increasing drone of traffic combined with his laboured breathing meant he could no longer hear the crew at all, let alone see them, and a strange idea took hold that they might have escaped into a parallel universe just to spite him. In reality, he had merely overtaken them while they'd been taking 'an easy' close into the bank and obscured by trees. But being in no state to reason calmly, he staggered onwards, seething inwardly, until coming to a halt beside the woman on the bridge.

At first, Hannah had been alarmed by his approach.

The unruly hair, the scratched face, the torn trousers and scuffed shoes doing nothing to offer reassurance and yet, she had a vague feeling of having seen this scarecrow before.

"Ha-have we missed them?" Anthony gasped by way of greeting.

"Who?"

"Ha-Halcyon!"

He was from the club. That was a relief anyway. But...

"Ass-associate of Perc's," continued the ragamuffin, proffering a hand.

So that was it.

"Straight from the outback?"

"Hah! That's not even funny!"

"Maybe you shouldn't talk for a moment in case you start hyper-ventilating."

"I've never let a little thing-like shortness of breath-stop me before."

"Evidently. Did you come from the club?"

"I wasn't at the meeting ,if that's what you mean. I had to wait outside like a dog!"

"Maybe we should start a club of our own!" she replied lightly before returning her eyes to the water. "Waifs and Strays? What do you think?"

Failing to get an immediate response, she glanced back again, giving him the full force of her smile as she did so and, much to her surprise, found the scarecrow strangely subdued. For, without knowing it, she'd uttered the first inclusive words he'd received since his arrival in London and disarmed him completely.

He was just about to tell her that he would be willing

to start anything she cared to mention when they both heard the beat of blades for the first time, very faint but drawing nearer.

First the white bow light flickered into view by Harrods Furniture Depository and then, suddenly, all eight blades lit up at once and glowed as they flew low above the water before dropping in again at the catch.

Then, as they exited at the end of the next stroke, they glowed again, creating eight skimming reflections as they did so.

Hannah and Anthony were both transported by the simple, yet wonderous spectacle. And, just for a moment, the Australian believed he had been admitted into that special parallel universe too.

*

Returning to the club after the outing, Perc had been relieved to find that Anthony was nowhere to be seen and, on that particular evening, out of sight really was as good as out of mind.

Walking back along the tideway he reflected on all that had taken place during the last few hours. The solitude was especially welcome because there was so much to take in. One extraordinary occurrence had seemingly followed so soon after another that it was hard to credit.

Firstly, he had spoken publicly for the first time and managed, or so he thought, to sound reasonably articulate. Not just that, but he had done so without losing his temper! Then there was the vote itself. And whilst he was not naive enough to expect attitudes would change overnight, he did sense that a major blockage had been cleared. And the picture of smooth conduits with free-flowing streams running through them inevitably conjured up the image of Baz. What a pity he hadn't been able to see them on the water that night. The boat had really *sung,* even Neil had said so. And what would he have made of the lights, what if he'd have been able to see them from Hammersmith Bridge, his bridge. Come to think of it, he'd have liked a peek from that vantage point himself. He was still wrestling with the difficulties of being in two places at once when his head hit the pillow.

It was perhaps hardly surprising then, that sometime later he was stirred from his slumbers by the clipped, polished tone of a familiar voice.

"What kind of sorcery is this?"

Turning, he saw Sir Baz, eyes twinkling as usual but focussed on something down beneath them. Following the direction of his gaze, Perc realised they were both standing on Hammersmith Bridge watching the approach of a rowing club eight.

"A craft illuminated by Jack-o-lanterns perhaps, or is it fireflies?"

Suddenly, the Australian tore his gaze away and tried to fix it on one of the bridge's stylish green painted stanchions. Was it vertigo that had brought the wave of nausea or the prospect of seeing himself and his crew as others did for the first time. That was an alarming idea for anyone, right? And yet, Sir Baz seemed so full of interest and excitement that he took a deep breath and forced himself to look down once more.

"Not of the sunlight, Not of the moonlight..."[11] mused his companion poetically.

"Well, er, all I can tell you is that each blade is wired to a battery inside the boat," explained the Aussie once he felt steady enough.

"Ah, yes, electricity, that's what it must be of course," beamed Baz.

"I was a great advocate for using it along the Victoria Embankment, but I never thought of using it *on* the water. Quite inspired. Quite inspired. One should always strive to push boundaries, don't you agree?"

"I wouldn't know, Sir," murmured Perc, feeling his life to be very small indeed when considered from their present vantage point.

"Ah, but you will, you will!" Baz re-joined heartily. "The right project will come along and then, whoosh, you'll be away. Away, I tell you. And now perhaps you can tell me something, is that one of the crews from along the Putney embankment?"

"Yes, it's Halcyon."

"Ah yes, so it is. I can just make out the coloured chevrons now. Very much like heraldic motifs, aren't they?"

The younger man readily agreed and then watched as Baz began to frown.

"Anything wrong?"

"No, no. Just trying to remember the next line of that Tennyson poem I mentioned. Yes, I have it now." And with that he reverted to the more distant and reflective tone

---

11   Alfred Lord Tennyson, 1809–1892, poet. Opening lines for final verse of *Merlin and The Gleam*.

he had used earlier. "*Over the margin, After it, follow it, Follow the gleam.*"

"I like that," said Perc after an appreciative pause. "It's something to live by."

"And to have *tried to live by it*, is something too, perhaps?" smiled the old man wistfully.

"More than something! Word from *over the margin* says you nailed it."

Baz twinkled at the compliment and then, with a bow of the head and a lift of his hat, he made his parting comment. "We will look out for each other again further upstream, yes?"

"We shall, good knight. We shall."

Chapter Twenty

"THE NEXT EVENT OF THE UPPER THAMES Regatta is the final of the Novice Eights, Halcyon vs Radcliff. Can we have both crews on the stake boats please?"

Halcyon paddled down from their waiting position just above Temple Island and, as they emerged from behind the trees, their white zephyr tops made it appear as if they had paddled directly from a bygone age. The club colours being restricted to just a single band of silk piping at the edge of each sleeve and the neck. Once in sight of the starting pontoon, Hannah steered them in before starting to straighten. "Touch her bow."

Gareth took the small, corrective stroke necessary, but with no back chat, each man knowing instinctively that the time for jokes was over. Any words that were spoken were murmured in hushed tones that mingled with the sounds made by trees and water.

"And again."

Once more Gareth kept the boat from drifting, keeping it in its lane as the river nudged and tugged playfully around it. It was teasing them just then, a subtle reminder that although it would never alter its nature on their account, it might just allow them the privilege of running with it for a while. If they were worthy, that is. It was the kind of understanding that one living thing has for another. Each knowing they are different yet recognising the shared bond of energy flowing between them, an energy they might even expend in joint revels for a spell.

Mark turned and grabbed Clive's shin, giving it an encouraging shake, a gesture the sixth man evidently appreciated, as he then smiled and his shoulders lowered visibly.

Perc, meanwhile, did a few neck exercises, glancing at the greenery on each side as he did so. The variety and jewel-like intensity of it all was startling to a man from inland Southwestern Australia. It felt as if he were in an illustration for a book, one of N.C. Wyeth's illustrations for *King Arthur* perhaps. The botanical detail adding veracity to the mythic exploits happening within their midst. Each plant and tree that he could see at that moment had a name and was contributing something to the scene.

Mark had told him that there were no small parts for actors, only shorter parts, but everyone was important to the whole. Knowing this, he felt a sudden wish to acknowledge this cast of thousands, an idea that was instantly followed by the sad realisation that he never could.

And yet, it might it be possible for one tiny bit of vegetation to represent the whole? How about – *comfrey?* A culinary herb that he had read about in a book about riverside walks. The name was derived from the Greek *to unite* and was formally thought to be helpful in the healing of wounds. Yes, that would do, it would have to do, for just then he heard Steady's voice, strangely spare and taut, cutting through the stillness. "Halcyon, prepare to die," was all he said, but it ended their collective reverie in an instant.

Hannah's arm came down and the next voice they heard was that of the umpire.

"Ready, set…"

All eyes were on Steady's blade, held poised for the first, crucial catch.

"Go!"

The start was good with Steady building up the length of each stroke. In fact, the start was so good the other crew seemed to believe Halcyon had gone early and would be called back, but as that call was never made, they realised they had allowed themselves to lose crucial momentum in the interim and were now going to have to play catch-up.

"Rhythm now," called Hannah and each man concentrated on making their blade work quicker and cleaner at the recovery. Fast hands had never been a problem for Perc, either in the ring or in the boat, and he spun them then like a man possessed.

"Don't tug, Gareth, use the legs." This from Dave who was somewhere on the towpath, though none of them allowed their eyes to wander away from the straight-ahead position, all too aware of the detrimental effect any shift of weight might make to their balance. Gareth, for his part, followed the instruction without question, or rather without trying to rationalise it. He simply kept slamming his legs down as hard as he could whilst saving his arms for the latter stages of each stroke.

As a consequence, the depth of his blade work promptly became more constant and effective, which was just as well as the Radcliff crew were creeping up on them. With her cox box mic turned high, Hannah knew her rival in the other boat would be able to hear her instructions and thus be quicker to respond whenever she made a call for extra power to pull further away from them. Fortunately, Halcyon were experienced enough by that stage of the summer to have devised a system of coded messages, seemingly innocuous chiding comments that every crew member understood meant something else entirely. It is also a fact, that even when a crew keeps its eyes in the boat, their peripheral vision quickly makes them aware of any other boat drawing parallel, and because of this they can sense when such a coded call is imminent. Its precise timing however is always down to the cox, though it may possibly be preceded by a telling look from the stroke man. Because of this fore knowledge, each man mentally prepared himself at that point for the big 'lift' they knew was coming. Every man breathing and rowing hard already but knowing they would soon be called upon to breathe and row even harder. For some there was a sense of exhilaration at the prospect, for others a sense of fear that they would be tested and found wanting. For Perc, who hitherto, had always faced his foes alone, the feeling of having seven other men fighting alongside him was the most liberating of his sporting life up to that point. And, although the reality of serious injury or even death was virtually non-existent compared the risks of being in the ring, he felt such a bond with his fellow oarsman just then that he truly believed he might sacrifice everything for their collective quest. Then it came. "Eyes in the boat," (get ready). "You're late two," (in two strokes.) "You're late two," (in one stroke). "You're *late*," (go all out, now!) And they did!

Every ounce of strength and energy was focussed on driving their boat forward, but they remained sitting tall as they did so, knowing full well that if they were to slump forward their strokes would shorten also.

After having drawn level, the confidence of the Radcliff crew had taken another hit whilst Halcyon, sensing the growing possibility of victory, continued to row better than ever as they approached the enclosures. But for all that, Radcliff were still only about half a length down.

"Go for home!" called Hannah, a cry that touched each of their respective cores.

They'd thrown in everything including the kitchen sink, bricks, mortar and roof tiles. Now it was foundations. Earth. Roots. Bedrock.

They could hear the Radcliff cox yelling too now. That crew can't, mustn't rob them of their just reward and yet they seemed to be moving forward again.

"Ten more strokes," called Hannah, and they dug in for ten more, but then there was eleventh stroke and a twelfth and then they lost count and realised she had lied to them. Why had she lied? Was it really *that* much further? It couldn't be. It was impossible to go on, but they just had to and through that impossibility they heard a hooter sound. It sounded far away, for another race perhaps, but there couldn't be two races on the course at the same time, so it must be for *their race* and they must have finished, but everyone still seemed to be paddling.

Then a voice, not their cox's voice, was saying something, but there wasn't enough oxygen in Perc's brain to comprehend. Someone called that Halcyon had won by a quarter of a length. Halcyon was *them*!

Then a voice that *was* familiar, Mike's voice. "Three cheers for Radcliff. Hip hip—"

How could he even talk after what they'd just been through?

"Hooray."

"Hip hip—"

The near equivalent of two punishing rounds back-to-back.

"Hooray."

"Hip hip—"

Wonder what the final time was exactly?

"Hooray."

Then they heard themselves being cheered by Radcliff in return and all they had to do during that was just breathe and listen, and as they did so, the euphoria of victory began to surge through their veins.

*

They were still buzzing after they had emerged from the presentation tent, which probably accounted for the way they all milled around each other afterwards. Everyone was so busy grinning and gazing at their trophies that they repeatedly looped back on themselves or bumped into crew mates.

"We won! We actually won something at last." Hannah was shouting to no one in particular.

"It *is* pretty amazing, isn't it?" agreed Perc, who happened to be nearest just then.

"And I just *love* my tankard."

"Even though it's only aluminium?"

"Why wouldn't I?"

"You seemed to have rather a lot of the stuff lying around on your patio already. Anymore might cause a glut on the market."

"No," she laughed. "Besides, I've been doing a lot of re-evaluating lately."

"I think we all have."

"And you helped."

"Me?"

"Yes. You *and* your friend Anthony."

"*Anthony!*"

The mere mention of the name was enough for Perc's throat to constrict. "That bloke's no friend."

"Associate then."

Perc shrugged. "Call him what you like, but I bet he peddled you a line, just the same."

"Of course, he did," she answered evenly. "But the figures didn't lie."

"Bad?"

"Shocking."

"What did I tell you?" replied the oarsman, slightly pacified. "Talking to him is like standing under the elephant's tail."

"But he does have a couple of assets…"

"*Right* under it."

"...And with a bit of clever debt restructuring. Anyway, it's all in the business plan I've drawn up. I'll give you a copy when we get back to the trailer."

"And what makes you think I'd even look at it?"

"Because," she replied, gently placing a hand on his arm, "it would be ungallant not to."

And with that she shrewdly moved on to share congratulations with the next person.

Perc stared after her for a moment before starting to head back towards the trailers.

Mike and his wife were just up ahead. Mike had his new son in his arms and was showing him his tankard, while his wife looked on and pushed the buggy. Tiny fingers and fingers that were full grown intertwined around the handle and there was a smile of delight on each face.

"Look at them," the woman smiled at Perc. "Two babies fascinated by a shiny new toy."

Perc did look, and the sight of the happy family group lifted his spirits again.

"Journey's end?" he asked lightly.

"Has to be," answered Mike. "At least until this one's a bit older."

Perc nodded, sensing the arrangement was the result of hard-won domestic compromise on both sides and wondering how he would've coped if asked to make a similar adjustment. Did he have it in him to steer a sensible course between the cross currents of everyday life the way Mike could?

"Mike can't go on trying to be a champion rower *and* a champion father," his wife elaborated as if she were able to read his mind and was wary of any challenge he might represent.

"It's wearing him out. It's wearing us *both* out, isn't it Mike?"

"Well, it *does* take up an awful lot of time," conceded the young father, diplomatically.

"Besides, I've got a blade mounted on the wall in our hallway, if ever I feel myself missing the boat too much, I can just take it down and give it a light feather on the carpet."

"On the crest of a weave, like?"

"Ha! Well, something like that."

They'd both grinned at the bad pun the way old friends will, but Perc's mind was still searching for an answer to the deeper question he'd asked of it.

Proving a point with your fists before a cheering crowd was one thing, he reflected once he'd left the trio behind, and striking a conciliatory tone in a meeting whilst surrounded by the moderating influence of crew mates was another. But what of his conflict resolution skills away from both crowd and crew? Did he have any? Had he ever had any?

The late afternoon sunshine bathed the field where the trailers were parked with a golden glow and Dave was already at work breaking down the eight, ready for transportation.

"Come on, you lot," he chided, "stop gassing and help me get this shell onto the trailer."

Steady climbed up to the front whilst others assisted from the sides.

"I was going to buy you all a drink back at the club, but the bar's going to be closed at this rate."

"I know for a fact that the bar never closes," winked Gareth.

"Me too," added Steady as he watched a female competitor doing cart wheels across the grass.

"There'll be a few pints of London Pride quaffed there tonight, that's for sure," said Mark, grabbing hold of a boat tie.

"Especially if Dave's paying," added the bow man.

"Only the first round," protested the coach, beginning to enter into the spirit of things.

"There's gratitude for you. His crew finally lose their novice status and he's only good for one measly shot. Unbelievable."

"Alright then, maybe two."

"That's better," replied Gareth, a little less indignantly.

"You can't stint at a christening, it's bad luck." Steady chimed in as the cartwheeling girl came nearer.

"But is beer really the right thing for a christening?" asked Sebastian. "How about a nice sparkling French wine instead?"

"Waste champers on this lot?" Mark retorted whilst tying a knot firmly.

"Ah well, maybe not," smiled the Frenchman with a sigh. "When in Rome, eh?"

"Rome? When in Halcyon!" corrected Clive.

At which point the cartwheeling girl, walking upright now, asked if anyone had a thirteen-milometer spanner she could borrow.

"Here, you can use mine," offered the stroke man jumping to the ground.

"Thanks, I'll bring it back," the girl replied with a grin.

"You'll never see that again," warned Gareth.

"Oh, yes I will," replied Steady watching her depart and resuming a familiar refrain with which the others quickly joined in: *"There are back water places all hidden from view, And quaint little islands just waiting for you, So I'll leave you right now to cast off your bow and go messing about on the river."*

By the end of it, Perc was in full voice too but broke off when Hannah handed him a black folder.

Glancing from the document back to the cox again, she directed his attention over to a spot near the bridge where Anthony was pacing.

"Aren't you coming back with us?" Gareth called. "There's room in my car."

"We came by train," the Australian shouted back, indicating Anthony with the kind of resigned tone one uses to explain illness or infirmity.

"Oh right, not sure I could manage two."

"Have a pint lined up for me. Hopefully I'll be there by the time you've got the boat off the trailer."

The bow man nodded as he secured the last of the ties.

*

"Seems like Old Father Thames was in kindly mood today," said Anthony, pointing up at the carved face on the bridge.

"Seems that way," the oarsman allowed whilst keeping the features of the keystone in view until they began ascending the steps.

They reminded him of Baz. Same long distinctive

nose and impressive facial hair. Not teased and manicured here, but seemingly moulded by the lapping waters below. As if the all the formalities of Victorian society had been stripped away to reveal the full force of the personality beneath. One force of nature co-existing peacefully beside another.

Downstream the engineer was undisputed champ, his work having redefined the shape and nature of the Thames to a remarkable degree, but here the river had played a part in the shaping too, making its presence felt just as surely as any other opponent worthy of the name. Each had somehow enhanced the other.

"Mind you, your crew looked pretty good too, coming down the straight."

"*Reach*! It's called Henley *Reach*."

"Coming down the *reach*, then."

Perc glanced at the picture perfectness of the view and let out a sigh. What he would've given to have been able to savour the moment alone for it seemed that, even then, it was already slipping away into the realm of memory.

"If only everyone else could be as benign," Anthony ventured tentatively.

"*Follow the gleam*," the river seemed to be saying.

"But you can never stand in the same river twice," Perc found himself saying in reply, unsure if he was answering the river, Sir Baz or the man standing beside him.

"So, just look at the document," urged his associate. "One should always have something sensational to read on the train."

Chapter Twenty-One

PERC LOOKED UP AT SPENCER AND ANTHONY. He was standing waist-deep in a freshly dug hole with a mound of orangey-red earth piled up high behind him.

"You were right, Spence," he said, holding up a section of broken terracotta. "The pipes *were* cracked. They were probably shoddy in the first place."

"Bastards," said Spencer.

"The run-off from the old mine workings must have leached into the soil so badly that now, whenever it rains, some of it gets flushed into the mains water supply."

"In such a hurry to get that ore out of the ground they couldn't be bothered to put anything decent back in its place," the old man spat in disgust.

"It'll take a while to check each section and replace with new, but we can do it, Spence."

"Do it so it so the water shines clear and pure again. Not just near the surface but deep down, where only the heart can see," added Perc, bright-eyed.

Spencer shook his head and looked at Anthony doubtfully.

"The money fellers won't like that. It's always get-rich-quick with them. Cutting corners."

"The money fellers know prospective clients won't settle for anything less," Anthony replied gravely. "The buyers we want to reach are discerning as well as affluent and in a challenging market we can't afford to cut corners if we want to see a return on our investment."

"Well, that's no bad thing, anyroad," conceded the old man.

Does that mean I'm officially appointed then?" asked Perc, clambering up out of the hole.

"The syndicate have accepted that they need someone permanently on-site to send off samples and supervise the contractors once they move in. Ethical Champion and Quality Assurance! That's how I sold the role to them. Just try not to be too pugnacious, OK?"

"I'll be the model of self-restraint," Perc grinned mischievously. "I've had lessons, remember?"

"I hope so, because I won't be able to get out here all that much from now on, I'll be too busy working with the architects and designers."

"Obviously," interjected Spencer.

"Yeah, well. Ideally, we want to be able to sell off plan, you see."

"Holiday homes," Spencer snorted dismissively.

"Holiday homes, reclamation, and re-greening," corrected Anthony before turning to Perc again.

"You'll be alright, won't you? And we'll still visit periodically with supplies."

"I'll be fine."

"Ever the lone wolf. Oh, and talking of supplies, this was waiting for you in the mailbox."

"Just a bill, probably," Perc shrugged disinterestedly whilst Anthony reached into his new briefcase. "Nah, too big for that, and from the UK too judging by the stamps."

Perc ripped off the end of the padded envelope, reached inside and pulled out a shiny, new, chromium-plated eggbeater, with a card tied to the handle.

"What does the note say?"

"*We'll beat again!*"

"Is that all?"

"That's all."

"How random is that?" Anthony asked as Perc turned the handle making the wheel and whisk components gleam in the sun.

"Maybe not so much," replied the new Ethical Champion winking at the old man. "After all, wherever the dreams go, the water follows and vice versa. Isn't that right, Spence?"

"I reckon so," came the terse reply.

"Well, if you two are going to start talking in riddles again…" muttered Anthony, readying to leave.

"No more riddles, just one last question for Spencer before he goes?"

"Shoot."

"Do you dream in colour or black and white?"

Spencer thought for a moment before starting to smile.

"Colour," he said at last. "Water colour!"

Bibliography

Ackroyd, Peter, *Thames Sacred River,* Chatto and Windus, 2007

Ackroyd, Peter, *Death of King Arthur,* Penguin Classics, 2010

Batchelor, John, *Tennyson, To Strive, To Seek, To Find,* Chatto and Windus, 2012

Bennett, Arnold, *The Card,* Penguin Modern Classics, 1975

Drabble, Margaret, *Arnold Bennett,* Weidfeld and Nicholson, 1974

Halliday, Stephen, *The Great Stink of London: Sir Joseph Bazalgette and the Cleansing of The Victorian Metropolis, Sutton Publishing Ltd, 1999*

Johnson, Robert, A, *He – Understanding Masculine Psychology,* Harper and Row, 1989

Kovacs, Charles, *Parsival – and The Search for the Grail,* Floris Press, 2002

Lanier, Sidney, *The Boy's King Arthur, Sir Thomas Malory's History of King Arthur and His Knights of the Round Table.* Edited for boys by Sidney Lanier, Hodder & Stoughton Ltd, London. Copyright 1880, 1917 by Charles Scribner's & Sons and 1908 by Mary Day Lanier for the United States of America.

May, Jessica, Podmaniczky, Christine, B, *N. C. Wyeth: New Perspectives,* Brandywine River Museum of Art, Chadds Ford,

Pennsylvania, Portland Museum of Art, Portland, Maine, In Association With Yale University Press, New Haven and London, 2019

Pearson, Heskith, *The Smith of Smiths,* Penguin Books in Association with Hamish Hamilton, 1948

Steinbeck, John, *The Acts of King Arthur and his Noble Knights,* Pan Books, 1979

Winn, Christopher, *I Never Knew That About The Thames,* Ebury Publishing, 2010

Acknowledgements

EVERYONE WILL HAVE THEIR OWN DEFINITION of what *The Gleam* is, and that's exactly how it should be.

It certainly isn't limited to the field of sport but exists in all kinds of endeavours and enterprises. And whilst it can be something that can be carried around inside one's head, it seems to shine brightest when working with others towards a common goal. Writing seems to be like that too. The theme or subject matter might be the author's alone, as is a large part of the process, but the real pleasure comes when seeking out and receiving external input and collaboration. This project has certainly been no different. However, before this book, or even the idea of it, there *was* a sport!

So, first and foremost, I want to thank all the people I've ever had the pleasure of rowing with and, also, all the people who coached, cajoled and encouraged me into a boat in the first place; coached, cajoled and encouraged from inside a boat once I was in it, and those who did all three from another boat running alongside.

Those days on the water were, and remain, genuinely magical and if only a small sense of the camaraderie and humour of those times comes across on the page, this book will have served its purpose.

When it comes to being specific, I want to express my appreciation to Terry Hackett who supported this water borne story from its inception and made crucial suggestions with regards to character development along the way. Edward Coke cheered it on at the halfway point and Steven Cook provided a much needed "lift" by sharing his own stories. Latterly, the enthusiasm of Andrew Walton provided the necessary impetus to get it "across the line" and out into the world for others to cast their eyes over. Being able to chat to Brian Callison was a privilege that won't be forgotten nor will Sue Browning's insight in pushing for more clarification and expansion in certain areas.

Every rower seeks that moment when their boat begins to 'sing' on the water and now, thanks to the sterling work of Linda Watts at Dejamus Limited in securing the necessary clearances, the Halcyon crew can now sing in print as well. Finding a Public Relations representative who also knows all about rowing is a rare thing indeed, but such a person exists in the indefatigable form of Zena Howard who, as always, puts heart and soul into every project she works on, this book being no exception. In fact, Zena starts even before the publication process begins!

Once those wheels start turning, as far as I'm concerned James Peak is the 'go-to' guy for audio book production and recording. Like all the best producers he has a great instinct about what is right for a project. Not just how it sounds but how it scans too. A latter day Merlin, if ever there was one!

Finally, my thanks go to Jonathan Keeble for bringing the audio version of the book to life so vividly. His delivery being the perfect aural equivalent of an N. C. Wyeth illustration: rich, robust and exiting. The perfect way, in fact, for this author's fictional quest to conclude.